Gina and Mike

The Yearbook Series

By Buffy Andrews

Gina and Mike

Copyright © 2013 by Buffy Andrews. All rights reserved.
First Print Edition: August 2013

Limitless Publishing, LLC
Kailua, HI 96734
www.limitlesspublishing.com

Cover: Eden Crane Designs
Formatting: Limitless Publishing

ISBN-13: 978-1492156512
ISBN-10: 1492156515

Dedication

To Tom, my forever love

Chapter 1

Gina

The bastard was dead.

I stared at the newspaper clipping that Mom had mailed me. I had read his obituary online, but seeing it on paper in front of me made it more real. Kind of like watching the Wicked Witch of the West melt in the "Wizard of Oz" – all the evil you loathe becoming a puddle of nothing.

Richard M. Smith, 61, was ushered into Heaven on Saturday, February 11, 2012, surrounded by his family at his home.

I'm pretty sure he went to Hell.

He was a loving husband, devoted father and dedicated coach.

1

He was the biggest asshole on this side of the Mason-Dixon Line. Maybe on the whole East Coast. Oh, what the hell, let's just say the entire country. You get the point, he was an A-S-S-H-O-L-E, and I hated him more than I've ever hated anyone in my life.

Mostly because he ruined it.

I grabbed my high school yearbook off the shelf in my office. Mom brought it on her last visit. She was cleaning out the basement, and it was among the things she didn't want to throw away or take to Goodwill.

I opened the book and read the message I've read so many times I know it by heart.

Gina,

To the best and sweetest girl any guy could have. You're super in every way and you mean everything to me, and don't ever forget that! You know I don't like to write because I can't express myself as well as if I would tell you but I'll try anyways. I love you very much and want our relationship to last! You're just a super girl, you care about me very much and I appreciate it because it makes me feel great inside, and I feel very lucky to have a girl as great as you. If I had to sum everything up about you in one word it would have to be amazing! It probably sounds dumb but that's the way it is. I just want to let you know that

I do love you and will do anything for you that you want me to.
   Love, Mike

I remember his black hair and curls. His five o'clock shadow in the middle of the day. The way his smile took up most of his olive face and the way his dark eyes danced when I walked into the room. I remember the first time he told me he loved me, and the first time we made love. Why is it that you never forget your first love? Maybe it's because it's the first person you gave your heart to, completely. The first time you were afraid to breathe for fear the moment would pass and you would miss some of the seconds. Life is seldom what we think it will be. Especially when you're seventeen and the biggest concern you have is whether someone has the same prom dress.

I ran into Mike once at the pizza shop in town. It was the day after Christmas, and I was home visiting my parents. I saw him as soon as I opened the glass door and the bell jingled. He stood at the counter, holding a baby bundled in blue. The sight washed over me like a damn wave that you never see coming until it's too late and you're face down eating sand. And just as you try to spit out the sand and stand up, you get knocked over again by the damn hot pizza smell that transports you back in time. Back to the night that you ate pizza in the corner booth that still has your names carved in the wood. The night you got drunk on the six-pack you took from your dad's stash in the garage. The night you made out in the woods and fell asleep naked intertwined like pretzels under a crescent moon.

He turned and saw me and then came the smile. His white teeth seemed even whiter, his smile broader. There was small talk and more small talk. About his marriage and baby and move across town.

What happened? What happened to all the plans we had? All the nights we spent lying under the stars sharing our dreams. The kind of house we'd live in, how many kids we'd have. What their names would be. What happened to us?

Life. That's what happened. One day comes after another and another and pretty soon you realize that yesterday was pretty damn long ago and that everything you had hoped for is never going to happen. You can't control it any more than you can control that big wave from getting stronger before it nails you. All you can do is prepare and hope that when it hits, you'll survive.

And hope that the secret you've kept all of these years doesn't drown you.

Chapter 2

1982

Gina

It's the spring of my senior year in high school, and I'm high on life. I have gotten into the college I wanted, everyone on the cheerleading squad is finally getting along and I have a super hot boyfriend who kisses like you wouldn't believe.

Sure, there are the occasional back-and-forth bitchiness among girlfriends and recurring arguments with Mom over my choice of clothes, but for the most part, life is unfolding in more or less the way I had expected it to.

Then came the night that changed everything. Like a stop sign that you see too late. You run the intersection and collide with an out-of-control car and your life is never the same.

There's just too much damage.

****

I was babysitting for my calc teacher, Mr. Smith, who was also Mike's baseball coach, and his wife, Lisa.

Lisa was a nurse at the hospital and worked nights so she could be home with their sons during the day. The oldest was three and the youngest was almost one.

It was a Thursday night. Normally Mr. Smith would be home, but Lisa had called earlier in the week to see if I could babysit so he could go out with friends. One of them was being deployed overseas and the guys wanted to get together one last time.

I wasn't crazy about Mr. Smith. The way his eyes jumped to my chest whenever he talked to me freaked me out. And he invaded my personal space like bees in a hive. It totally made me feel icky. He'd stand behind me and look over my shoulder as I was doing math problems and I'd swear it was just so he could look down my shirt. I had seriously thought about writing across my breasts, "Fuck You" upside down in black marker so he'd get the message without me having to say anything. And, I have to admit, I liked the idea of letting him know that I knew what a creep he was.

But I didn't have anything planned, and Mike had to work at the grocery store, so I agreed to babysit. Besides, I could use the money. I was just beginning to realize how expensive college was going to be, and I needed every cent I could make and every scholarship I could get.

The boys were sound asleep, and I was doing homework at the kitchen table when I heard the garage door go up. It was 11:13. As I packed my backpack, Mr. Smith walked into the kitchen.

He stumbled and grabbed the kitchen counter to steady himself. "How's my favorite babysitter tonight?"

He reeked of beer and cigarette smoke. His eyes were glassy and his speech slurred. I had never seen him like this, and it scared me. I didn't like the way he was looking at me, with his tongue hanging out like some damn dog waiting for a treat. I wanted to get out of there as fast as I could, but it meant walking past him to get to the back door.

I grabbed my backpack and held it in front of me like a shield. "Well, I'd better get going. Mom's expecting me."

As I walked past him to get to the door, he grabbed me by the waist and pulled me in. "Where ya gone so fast?" he slobbered into my neck. "Why not hang around for awhile?"

I pulled away. "I don't think that's a good idea."

He jerked me back. "It's a great idea. And I got something that you want."

He forced my hand on top of his bulging crotch.

"Feel that. That's bigger than Mike's. I know because I've seen his in the locker room. He's a rookie. A hot redhead like you deserves someone who knows what to do with his cock."

I yanked my hand away. I wanted to scream. I should have screamed. But I didn't want to wake up the boys, and I really thought I could get away and handle everything. But just when I thought I had freed myself, I was on the cold vinyl floor. Mr. Smith grabbed a floral dishtowel off the counter and gagged me with it. He pulled my long hair as he tied it around my head. I tried to kick him but he just laughed. He yanked down his jeans and blue boxers. His hard penis popped out. He straddled me like a horse. I squirmed as he ripped off my bikini underwear and sniffed them before tossing them aside.

"Umm. Your pussy smells sweet. Let's give it a treat."

He pulled up my sundress and forced his fingers inside me before ramming into me like a round peg being forced into a square hole. Pain coursed through my body. I shook my head and tried to wiggle free. He pinned my arms to the floor.

"Tight bitch. And I know you're not a virgin."

I flailed, trying to get away. But he just kept ramming me. Tears soaked my cheeks. The dishtowel gag stopped them from dripping off my face. My insides hurt. I felt so dirty and violated. It seemed like he took forever before he pulled out and came all over my stomach. Some of the semen got on my new sundress. When he was done, he got off of me and threw me a towel to wipe off my stomach. I could feel sour acid inching up my throat as I cleaned myself off. The semen smell was over powering.

Smith wiped his mouth on his red and blue polo shirt. "Now that's how a bitch like you needs to be fucked. And, tell anyone what happened and Mike will pay for it."

He took off the gag.

I sprung to my feet and my sundress fell down over my sticky midsection. The wet spot on the sundress touched my thigh. I grabbed my backpack. "You're a fuckin' pig!" I ran as fast as I could out the door and to my car. I left my pink underwear behind along with my innocence – the world was more screwed up than I could have ever imagined.

I stood under the hot shower and scrubbed my skin until it burned. But no matter how much I scrubbed, I couldn't escape the smell of beer and smoke, the sound of his sweaty skin slapping against mine and the pain of him tearing me apart inside. I hated him, and I knew that I would never be the same. I kept touching my stomach, imagining that the globs of semen were still there and that no matter how hard I tried to wipe them away, they'd keep resurfacing. I felt dirty and ashamed.

I was scared. I thought about telling Mom but I didn't think she'd believe me. She thought the Smiths were a "lovely family." More importantly, I didn't want to do anything that would hurt Mike. And Smith said that if I told anyone, Mike would pay. I couldn't do that to Mike. Baseball was everything to him. He had pitched varsity since he was a freshman and had hoped for a baseball scholarship to his dad's alma mater.

Mike wanted to make his dad proud. His dad had just been diagnosed with Lou Gehrig's disease and the family was devastated. Knowing that his dad was going to die made Mike even more determined to attend the college his dad did. But it was a private school and very expensive. Mike needed the scholarship to help pay his way. So I wasn't about to let Smith jeopardize Mike's scholarship chances by benching him or pulling some other screwed up move.

I stuffed my stained sundress into a plastic bag and hid it under my bed. I was never going to wear it again. Ever! I wrapped myself in the red and yellow Snow White blanket I had since I was a little girl. I remember begging Mom to buy it. I must have been about five at the time. Twelve years later, it still comforted me in a way I couldn't quite explain. It was like being wrapped in childhood sweetness, a protective armor made of hugs and kisses and everything good.

Mom knocked on the door and walked in. "Everything, OK?"

I looked up from my book. "Yeah, why?"

"Just that you didn't say anything when you got home. You came right up here. Hungry?"

I shook my head. "I had pizza with Alex and Andrew."

"Get all your homework done?"

"Yeah."

"I guess it was good that you babysat for the Smiths tonight," Mom said.

I jerked my head. "Why?"

"Just that Mr. Smith can help you with your calc, since you've been having trouble and all."

"No."

"No what?" Mom asked.

"I don't need his help. I wouldn't want his help. I'm doing fine in his class."

As soon as I said it I heard the razor sharp anger in my voice.

Mom tilted her head in confusion. "Are you sure everything's all right?"

"Positive." I closed my book. "I'm just tired. Too many late nights."

I waited until Mom left before I grabbed my journal out of my antique mahogany nightstand. I wanted to write about what happened. How I felt. But I was afraid that if I wrote it down on paper, it would live forever. And I didn't want it to live forever. I wanted it to be gone.

Besides, what if someone found my journal and read it? That would be even worse. No. It had to be my secret. No one could ever know. It had to be my secret.

Forever.

***

The next day was Friday. I would have feigned being sick but I didn't want to make up the physics exam I had been studying for all week. I liked when I didn't have to study on a weekend for a Monday test and could just relax. The only good thing about the day was that Smith wasn't at school. I hoped that his bald head felt like a sumo wrestler was sitting on it.

On my drive to school, I stopped at the mini mart and stuffed my sundress into the outside trashcan. When I bought the bright yellow dress, I thought it was beautiful, the color of Mom's flowering buttercups in spring. I couldn't wait to wear it. Now, the dress represented everything I hated. I could still smell Smith's stink on it and it made my stomach lurch.

I knew that I owed Mike an apology. When he called after work, I didn't hang on the phone long. He kept asking what was wrong and the more he asked the more irritated I became. We ended up arguing over which Girl Scout cookie was the best. So incredibly stupid, I know.

I was stashing my physics book in my locker when I saw Mike out of the corner of my eye. His hands were behind his back, and I could tell he was holding something.

When he walked up, he kissed me on the cheek and I jerked.

"You OK?" he asked.

I nodded.

"How was the physics exam?"

"Totally sucked, but at least it's over."

He held out the box of Thin Mints he had been hiding behind his back, and his lopsided smirk tumbled into a smile. "It's a peace offering." His eyebrows raised in exclamation. "Your favorite."

I felt the corners of my mouth turn up. A smile slid onto my face before I could stop it.

Mike's little sister, Alice, was selling Girl Scout cookies, which is how we got into the pathetic fight in the first place. Mike had to drive Alice around after school to deliver orders. He brought it up so I'd know he wouldn't be able to come over to my house after school.

I took the box of cookies. "Thanks. Sorry for being such a bitch last night."

Mike brushed my long hair out of my face. "Are you sure you're all right? You look tired."

"I am."

"Not too tired for later, I hope."

"No. I'll be ready at 7."

We had plans to go for ice cream and then to the woods to make out. We hadn't been together for a while because of Mike's work schedule. Before last night, I couldn't wait to be with him, to be wrapped in his arms and next to the body I knew so well. Now, I wasn't so sure. I hoped that when it was just the two of us, everything would be OK, that it would fall back into place like nothing had happened. But I knew that I wouldn't know until that moment came. My heart shifted into overdrive just thinking about it.

The bell rang and Mike kissed me again before heading off for the last class of the day. I had English class, and I was hoping that the teacher was in one of her talking moods. Sometimes, she wasted an entire period telling stories about when she was a kid. There was this one guy who was really good at luring her into monologues when no one felt like working. I would have to tell Eric that today was one of those days and see what he could do.

"Hey, Gina. Wait up."

I turned around to see my best friend, Sue. A hair over five feet tall, she's built like a gymnast and definitely has the energy of one. Everyone calls her Tigger, because she always seems to be bouncing from place to place.

"How come you didn't call me back last night?"

"I had to babysit, remember?"

"Yeah, I know. But you could have called afterward. I had something really important to tell you."

"Like what?"

Sue looked around to see if anyone was super near us and then leaned in close to me. "Like Dave broke up with Diane and now she doesn't have a date to the prom and she bought her dress already."

My eyes popped like champagne corks. "Really? But they've been together forever."

"Yeah, as long as you and Mike. Maybe a little longer."

"How's Diane?"

"OK. She said she saw it coming. She said that Dave was ignoring her and acting weird. Dave, on the other hand, acts like he's won the freakin' lottery. Jerk!"

"So what's Diane going to do?"

"Take her dress back. She said that even if a guy asked her to the prom that she wouldn't want to go because she'd feel like he was only asking her because he pitied her or something. And she doesn't want to be pitied."

"What about Dave?"

"Word in the hall is that he's going to ask a ninth-grader. Some girl he's apparently had his eye on all year. "

"Ouch."

"Yeah, tell me about it. It totally sucks for Diane."

I couldn't help but thinking how trivial the whole Dave and Diane saga was compared to what I was dealing with. I mean, I was raped. Raped by one of my teachers. I couldn't tell Mom. I couldn't tell my best friend. I couldn't tell anyone. About the only thing I could do was stay as far away from asshole Smith as I could.

I couldn't avoid going to class, but I could avoid babysitting for him. Mom would wonder why I stopped babysitting for the Smiths, so I'd have to come up with good excuses. Then again, maybe the asshole will tell his wife that I'm a lousy babysitter and not to call me anymore. The worst part about this colossal mess is that I really liked Alex and Andrew. I'll miss them, and I'm pretty sure they'll miss me.

Eric was sitting at his desk right inside the door when I walked into English class. I stopped and whispered into his ear. He nodded, and I knew he would see what he could do.

Chapter 3

Gina

Eric charmed Mrs. Hoffman, who was more round than she was tall, and it wasn't long before she was decades deep telling a story from her childhood. She was the type of person who told you every little detail. Sometimes, she got so caught up in the details that she'd forget where she was in the story and someone would have to remind her. Today, she talked about the big red and white Coca-Cola cooler at this store near her childhood home.

"And you'd flipped back the lid, reach into the ice-cold water and pull out a bottle of soda," she said, rubbing her chubby hands together as if she was warming them. "There was a bottle opener attached to the front of the cooler. I'd wipe the wet bottle off with my shirt, pop off the cap and drink it fast so I wouldn't have to share it with my sister."

Of course Eric, who looked like Clark Kent minus the glasses, did his usual good job of asking questions to keep the story going. Mrs. Hoffman thought he asked the questions because he was genuinely interested in what she had to say and for that, he was her forever favorite.

Today, he asked her what kinds of soda they had back then and she went on to talk about Frostie root beer (her favorite).

"I can still picture the bottle cap. It was red, white and blue with a picture of a man with a mustache and beard," she said. "Back then, you'd get a penny for every glass soda bottle you returned to the store. Of course, I always returned the bottle because I could then buy a piece of penny candy."

It was at this point – in the middle of her describing the red, white and blue bottle cap – that I zoned out. Her details were like sleeping pills. The more she fed me the sleepier I got.

When I jerked awake, Mrs. Hoffman was describing how the store owner chewed tobacco.

"This man, who was probably in his late 60s or early 70s. Oh, and did I tell you that he lost the tip of his middle finger in a meat slicer when he was quite younger? Yes, well, anyway he did. Uh, where was I?"

"He chewed tobacco," Eric said.

"Yes, the tobacco. Well, old Mr. Mahoney would open the store door and spit out the big, juicy wads of tobacco. And if I walked to the store in bare feet, which I often did in the summer. I hated shoes. Still do. I'd have to be careful not to step on the wet wads."

"Did you ever step on one?" Eric asked.

Thank God the bell rang because her description of stepping on a slimy black blob was making me want to puke.

"Thanks, Eric," I whispered as I walked past him. "The tobacco wads were a little too much, though."

He smiled. "I didn't feel like discussing *The Iliad* either so it was all good."

When I got to my locker, Sue was waiting for me. "You didn't forget, did you?"

I had no idea what she was talking about.

She put her hands on her hips. "Prom dress shopping. You said you'd go with me."

"Crap. I did forget. I promised Mike that I would be ready by 7 so I need to be home by 6."

"Well, that gives us a couple of hours. We can get one shop in. How about Bridal Bliss?"

"Sure."

I really didn't feel like going dress shopping with Sue, but I knew how excited she was about this year's prom. She really, really, really liked Ron. Last year's prom was more of a friend affair. Sue needed a date and Keith needed a date and they were friends so they decided to go together. This year was a different story. She was really hot for this basketball player we met when we cheered at St. Francis Catholic High. We saw Ron in the hallway after the game and he asked Sue for her number. They had been hot and heavy ever since. She was even thinking about going the whole way with him.

When we got to the bridal shop, there were rows and rows of dresses in every color and style imaginable. Sue had brought a teen fashion magazine (prom edition) and showed the page she had paper clipped to the clerk.

"I'd like something like this," she said, pointing to a picture of a long powder blue gown with sequins on the bodice.

"I think I have something similar," the clerk said. "Follow me."

I leaned against the floral wallpaper wall as Sue tried on dress after dress. I was glad I had my prom dress and all of the accessories bought. Mom and I had taken care of that a few weeks ago. I chose a pink gown that I absolutely adored as soon as Mom pulled it off the rack. Better yet, it was on sale because the style was being discontinued. So I got my dress for half of its original price. I loved bargains.

"On a scale of one to ten, with ten being the best, what's this dress?" Sue asked, turning in a circle. It was a mint green gown with poufy sleeves.

"A six."

"I agree. The dress has to be a ten."

She held up the first dress she tried on. It was a pale yellow with a fitted bodice, scoop neckline and elbow length sleeves that gathered into sleeve bands. "This one reminds me the most of Princess Di's."

I agreed; it was the closest. Sue was fascinated by the whole Princess Di and Prince Charles love affair. The day of the wedding, she got up super early so she could watch the entire ceremony on TV. She was determined to find a prom dress that had some resemblance to Di's dress. The clerk wrote all of the information down on a card for Sue, who decided to check a few more shops before making her final decision. By the time I got home, I was exhausted.

I had an hour before Mike picked me up. I set my alarm so I could lie down for twenty minutes before hopping into the shower.

I had tossed and turned the night before. The rape played over and over in my mind. And like a movie you watch repeatedly, new details emerged that you saw but had forgotten or pushed aside. Like the dark, dime-size mole on Smith's torso between his belly button and pubic hair.

I thought about what I could have done, what I should have done to stop Smith. I was mad at myself for not fighting him harder, and I vowed to take classes to learn how to defend myself better.

I never said anything to Mike, but I wasn't exactly thrilled when I got Smith for calc. His wife was nice enough. I actually met her through church. She sang in the choir with Mom and when she was looking for a babysitter a couple years ago, Mom suggested me. Of course, that was before I had Smith for class and Mike was my boyfriend.

Mike licked his dripping ice-cream cone. "What's wrong with you tonight? I can tell something's bothering you."

I bit my lower lip. God I wanted to tell him, but I couldn't. For starters, Mike would confront Smith and probably kill the bastard and end up in jail. And second, what proof did I have? Zilch! Maybe I should have kept the sundress just in case I'd change my mind. But Mr. Smith's semen on my dress wouldn't prove that he raped me. It would just prove that somehow his semen got on my dress. The how was the important part and Smith would probably turn it around and I'd come out looking like a slut who came on to him.

"Sorry I'm not my usual self. Guess I just have a lot on my mind," I told Mike.

"Like what?"

"Just school stuff."

"Like the physics exam?" Mike asked.

"Yeah."

"I'm sure you did fine. Probably got an A. Oh. Almost forgot. Did you hear about Dave and Diane?"

"Sues told me. I can't believe it."

Mike wiped his mouth with a napkin. "It wasn't a complete shock to me. Dave's been talking about that Caryn chick for awhile."

"The ninth-grader?"

Mike nodded. "Dave says he'll get to third base on the first date."

"You're a pig."

"Hey, I didn't say that, Dave did."

"Yeah, but you repeated it," I told him.

"To you."

"Still..."

"Man, you are a little edgy. Let's get out of here."

I grabbed my purse and followed Mike to his beat-up brown sedan with coffee-stained interior. By the time we got to our making-out spot, my heart revved into overdrive.

Mike turned off the car and looked at me. "Gina, you're shaking." He cupped my hands in his. "If you don't want to make out, it's OK. I'll take you home."

"No," I said. "I want to be with you."

Mike leaned over and we kissed. Gentle kisses rolled into urgent ones. And after a few minutes of deep kissing we grabbed his blue sleeping bag out of the trunk and headed into the woods. Our making-out spot was under a towering oak tree that scratched the sky.

Mike unzipped the nylon bag the entire way so it was like a double-size blanket. The plaid liner faced up. I lay down beside him and we started kissing again. Mike reached under my shirt and I flinched.

"Relax, baby," he whispered into my ear.

He unhooked my bra and I helped him unbutton my shirt. I tried to relax, but as Mike's mouth trailed down my neck onto my chest, my heart raced. I closed my eyes. Maybe if I pictured the beach that would help me relax. It worked when I was in the dentist chair and he was drilling a cavity. But picturing the beach didn't work. When I closed my eyes, I saw Smith's bushy mustache and bald head and dime-size mole and heard him say, "Tight bitch."

I stiffened as Mike kissed one breast and then the other. He moaned. "Oh, Gina, baby. I missed you."

I stiffened.

Mike stopped his trail of kisses. "Tell ya what," he said, pushing back the strands of hair that fell across my face. "Not sure what's going on with you, but I'm just going to hold you. We don't have to do anything. Just let me hold you."

I nodded. "Sorry."

He lay on his side, and I backed up as close as I could to him. He slipped his bulging bicep around me and pulled me even closer. His bare chest was against my naked back. I could feel his warm breath on the back of my neck.

"You know that I love you, right Gina?" he whispered. "I love you more than anything."

I reached down and pulled up his pitching hand and kissed it. "I know. And I love you, too."

I hated Smith. I hated him for what he did and for how he made me feel. I hated myself for allowing it to happen. If only I would have said no to babysitting. If only Mike hadn't been working that night then we would have been together. If only, if only. I hated those two words, too.

I loved Mike. I wanted to be with him. I wanted to marry him and have his kids, but every time he touched me I became defensive, like he was trying to hurt me. But Mike would never hurt me. He loved me. I kept telling myself that I would get better; that these feelings I had would pass. That I just needed time. And I also realized how much I was dreading Monday. I was scared to death of Smith and how he would react the first time he saw me. The dread shrouded me like a morning fog, only this fog never gave way to sunshine.

"You're not mad, are you?" I asked Mike as he pulled in front of my house.

He turned off the car. "I'm not mad; I just don't understand what's going on. We haven't been together for a while and I know that you were looking forward to tonight as much as I was. And then the way you acted, like you didn't want to be with me or something."

I looked at Mike with his puppy dog droopy eyes. His smile had run away from his face. I hated that I was disappointing him. "It's not you. I swear. I just have some things I need to work through. Things I'm not ready to talk about."

He slammed the steering wheel. "But we tell each other everything."

I sighed. "You're right. We usually do. But..."

"But what, Gina?"

Mike was practically shouting and it startled me. I wasn't used to him raising his voice.

"You just have to trust me on this one, Mike. I love you. It has nothing to do with you or my feelings for you. They haven't changed. They'll never change. But I need to work out some things and you have to let me and trust that I love you more than anything."

He reached over and lifted my chin. "Damn. OK. I'll give you time, but I still wish you'd let me know what's going on inside that beautiful red head of yours."

I smiled. "Just remember that I love you."

We kissed long and deep before I said goodbye, got out of the car and walked inside.

****

I sat in church and listened to Pastor Greg's sermon about Jesus going into the wilderness for forty days. He said that we all have our wilderness stories, times in our lives when things didn't go right.

"Some of you might be in the wilderness right now," he said. "Jesus went into the wilderness as a carpenter's son and came out as the Messiah."

He told us to find meaning in our wilderness, glimmers of grace.

I was definitely in the wilderness, and I was not seeing any glimmers of grace. And I was pretty sure that when I came out of the wilderness, I wasn't going to be changed for the better.

Screw the whole wilderness saga, I thought. There was no way I was going to find meaning in a wilderness that I had been forced into by a drunk teacher who I was pretty sure was also high on something.

Sue found me after church and asked if things went better on Saturday with Mike. I didn't tell her about the rape, only that Mike and I were having a tough time. Saturday was more or less a repeat of Friday. Mike picked me up after work and we went to the movies and then to the woods. He ended up just holding me like the night before.

"You're not going to end up like Dave and Diane, are you?" Sue asked.

My eyes spat fire. "It's not that bad. Just a little rough right now."

"OK. Just checking. Cause I really like Mike."

"Me, too," I said. "Sometimes maybe too much."

****

I wasn't prepared to see the bastard at the gas station on Monday, but just as I rammed the nozzle into my gas tank he slid into the pump in front of me. I didn't look at him. I looked at the ground and then at the pump and then back down at the ground. When the nozzle clicked, I hung it up, screwed on the cap and headed inside to pay.

When I came out, Smith was waiting by my car. He had a doozy of a black eye.

"Look, Gina," he said. "About Thursday night. Sorry that happened. Guess I got a little out of hand."

"A little? No, I'd say a lot, you fuckin' pig. And don't you ever think about touching me again."

He kicked the ground. "Well, remember what I said. Keep what happened between you and me and Mike gets to be a star. Don't, and he might just have the worst baseball season ever."

My eyes threw daggers. I knew I had to be brave. I couldn't appear weak, even though I was shaking and felt fear choking me. I needed to let him know that I meant business. I had practiced what I would say all day Sunday if and when I had the chance to confront him. I just had to keep calm and not lose my nerve.

"First, I hate your fuckin' guts and the only reason I'm not saying anything to anyone is because I love Mike and want the best for him. But I have another condition."

He tilted his badass bald head. "What?"

"I get an A in your class."

"But you're barely passing."

"Guess that means I'll be your miracle student."

He twisted his lips into a smirk. "No one would believe you anyhow."

"Fine with me if you want to take that chance."

He kicked the ground again. "OK. You get the A. Slut!"

He walked toward the store to pay for his gas and I sped away as fast as I could. When I could no longer see the store in my rear-view mirror, I took a huge deep breath. I couldn't believe what I had just pulled off. Somehow I was believable. Even if Smith wouldn't have agreed to the A, I still wouldn't have told anyone what he had done because of Mike. But at least now I didn't have to worry about calc any more. I got an A.

Chapter 4

Mike

I hate funerals but Mom shamed me into going. She reminded me, as if I needed to be reminded, that if it hadn't been for Coach Smith, I wouldn't have gotten a full ride to Madison. And, if I hadn't gotten into Madison, I wouldn't have met Lisa my senior year. And If I wouldn't have met Lisa my senior year, I wouldn't have Jack. And Jack is the best thing in my life. He's the only good thing that ever came out of my marriage to Lisa.

When Jeremy called and told me Coach dropped over dead while mowing the lawn, I about had a heart attack. Turned out, that's exactly what happened to Coach. His wife was looking out the kitchen window when she saw him fall to the ground. By the time she reached him, he was dead. Damn. When your time's up, it's up. No negotiating. No pleading. Nothing. You're dead. End of story.

Guess you never know for sure how your life's going to turn out. I thought I was going to marry my high school sweetheart, Gina McKenzie. God, I loved that girl. And I thought she loved me. Sometimes when Jack's over at Lisa's, I dig out the old yearbook and read what she wrote in it.

Mike,

To the love of my life forever and always. Thank you for loving me and for always being there for me. When we're old and gray, we can get out our yearbooks and read what we wrote to each other. That'll be fun. Remember, you said you'd love me even when I'm old and wrinkled and have white hair and false teeth.

Love you always, Gina

Yep. That was the plan. We'd marry and grow old together. After Gina dumped me, I swore off girls. Thought I'd never get married. The breakup happened the summer before our freshman year in college. I'm still not sure I know what happened.

****

1982

One day we were great and the next day we weren't. I tried talking to Gina about it, but the more I tried, the more distant she became. The night of the prom was the beginning of the end. We went to the after party at Jeremy's house and everything seemed great until we went to the woods to make out.

It was like Gina didn't want me to touch her. I tried doing everything she liked, but she kept pushing my hand away or turning her head. When I tried to slip off her bikini underwear, she pulled them back up. When I unhooked her bra, she seemed like she was pissed about it. She definitely wasn't the Gina I knew – and loved. Something had happened, but damn if I knew what? And Gina sure as hell wasn't talking about it. She had been acting this way for weeks.

"Gina, baby, what's wrong?" I asked, rubbing my thumb over her full lips. "It's been so long since we made love. I think I'm going to explode I want you so bad. Is it me? Don't I turn you on anymore?"

Gina bit her lower lip. "It's not you."

"Well, damn, Gina, I'm the only one here so it's tough not to think it's me. There was a time when kisses down your neck and chest would have had you clawing the shirt off my back. Now you're colder than the deep freezer at work. What the hell am I supposed to think?"

Gina sat perfectly still on the sleeping blanket, wringing her hands, and staring straight ahead. She didn't want to look at me. She was bathed in soft moonlight and I swear she looked like an angel. It killed me not to be able to touch her in the way I wanted to.

"I just need time."

"Time for what? You've been saying that for weeks, and I've given you weeks. But you just become more and more distant. It's like I'm losing you and I don't know what to do to stop it. At first I thought that whatever was going on, you'd tell me about it eventually. You always do. Well, did. Anyway, you haven't and I know it's still on your mind."

"I'm sorry, Mike. I'm trying."

She turned and looked at me and I searched her glassy eyes, looking for something I knew I wasn't going to find.

"That's just it," I said. "You used to not have to try. It just happened. We were great together."

I'm not sure why it didn't hit me before, but I thought maybe Gina was pregnant. She was on the pill, but still.

"You're not pregnant, are you?" I asked.

Gina shook her head. "Jesus, no. It's not that."

I let out a heavy sigh.

"I wish it were that," she whispered.

"What you'd say?" I asked.

"Nothing."

"You said you wish you were pregnant. I heard you," I told her.

"Well, if you heard me then why'd you asked what I said?"

"Christ, Gina. I'm not ready to be a dad. But if that would be better than whatever's going on, whatever's going on must be pretty damn bad."

Gina didn't say anything, but I could tell by the way her body stiffened that she was uncomfortable.

"You're not gay, are you?"

She jabbed her elbow into my side.

"Just checking cause, you know, you don't seem to want me. Or this."

I took her hand and placed in on my crotch and you would have thought that I had cut off her arm.

Gina jumped up. "What the fuck do you think you're doing?"

I stood up and tried to hug her but she turned away. "Gina, baby. I'm Sorry. I didn't mean."

"You didn't mean? You didn't mean? You think I'm a whore, don't you? Don't you? A whore. A lousy whore that's too tight..."

And she collapsed on the sleeping bag and rolled up in a ball and sobbed so loud I thought for sure the whole state could hear her. I laid beside her and gently put my arm around her, testing first to see if she would allow it. When it seemed like she was OK with it, I wrapped my arm around her and pulled her tight against my chest so that my heart beat against her back.

"Hush, baby, hush," I whispered. "Nothing's ever that bad that we can't talk about it." I kissed the top of her head and squeezed her gently. "Oh, baby, please. Please tell me what's going on inside that gorgeous red head of yours."

Gina sniffed and turned so our heads were facing each other on the blanket. The moonlight provided enough glow that I could see her blotchy red face. I brushed her hair away from her eyes.

She bit her lip. "I'm in the wilderness right now and I need to find my way out. "

"Oh, baby. What the hell are you talking about? We're in the woods. Our woods. Our make-out, happy place woods. This isn't a wilderness."

Gina shook her head. "I didn't mean it literally, Mike. It means that I'm having a tough time with something that I can't talk about. It's my journey and you can't come with me or help me. I need to find the way on my own. But please believe me when I say it's not your fault, it's not anything you did. I love you. I will always love you."

****

I was having a terrific baseball season. I had never pitched better, and college recruiters came to the games. Coach Smith was a big help. Some of the guys teased me about being his golden boy. It was true, he seemed to be paying more attention to me this year, but I wasn't about to complain. Coach was helping me get into Dad's alma mater. And, with dad's Lou Gehrig's diagnosis, getting into Dad's alma mater was even more important to me. I wanted to make Dad proud. I was his only son, and he always talked about me going to his school. I didn't want to disappoint him.

As great as baseball was, my relationship with Gina sucked. Big time. She never missed a game and when we went out, I always waited for her to make the first move. We never got past second base, and when you're used to hugging home, second base just doesn't cut it.

It wasn't so much that we didn't have sex, although I admit I missed the sex; it was that we didn't really talk anymore. I missed the closeness we once shared. I missed knowing everything there was to know about Gina. I missed knowing what she was thinking every minute of every day. I missed her.

Sometimes, I'd catch her staring at a spot in the distance and I'd know that her mind was in another place. I wanted the old Gina back and became frustrated that no matter what I tried, she didn't come back. It was like having the best present in the world and watching it disintegrate a little each day. Piece-by-piece; day-by-day; week-by-week.

It was no excuse, but one night Gina stayed home from a party at Jeremy's house. She was sick. I got pretty wasted and started making out with this chic, Patty Monroe. I knew Patty always had the hots for me. It was one of those things you can just sort of tell.

Patty's boobs always looked like they were about to pop out of her tight shirts. Her cleavage was as steep as the Grand Canyon, and she leaned over my desk every chance she got in math class.

I was sitting alone on the wooden bench by Jeremy's pool when Patty strutted out, wearing this too tight purple sundress that hugged her ass. She sat down beside me, tossing her long blonde hair back and licking her lips like those girls did in the porn movies Jeremy and I watched the other week. He found them in his dad's secret stash. I had too much to drink and was horny as hell and one thing led to another. We ended up in Jeremy's bedroom and things got out of hand. Fast. So fast that before I knew it Patty and I were half naked rolling on the floor getting carpet burns.

There was a knock at the door and before I could answer, Gina's best friend, Sue, had barged into the room and flicked on the lights. "Michael Parker, get your ass out of here, now!"

Sue pointed at Patty. "And you, you cheap bitch. If I ever see you so much as look at Mike, I'll flatten your tits and twist that head of yours into a pretzel."

Patty got dressed faster than a pit crew changes tires.

"I think I'm gonna be sick," I said.

"Good. I hope you get real sick," Sue said. "Serves you right. Cheating on my best friend like that. What the fuck were you thinking?"

Sue grabbed the black trashcan by the desk and sat it in front of me.

Blech! I coughed. *Blech!* "God my head is spinning. I feel so dizzy." *Blech!*"

"And I hope you feel even worse tomorrow. Now get dressed. I'm taking you home."

****

I had one hell of a hangover the next day, and I really wasn't up for listening to Sue when she called to ream me out – again. Her mouth ran like a river the night before during our drive home from Jeremy's. And today, it still ran like a river but was accented with ice-cold white caps that tossed me about like I was a toy.

"And another thing, Mike. If you ever, and I mean ever, so much as look at another girl, I will kick you in the cock so hard you'll never be able to use it. Do you hear me?"

"Yes. I'm sorry. I screwed up. I don't know what got into me. You know that's never happened before, Sue."

"And it better not ever happen again. I'm not going to tell Gina. I don't want to hurt her and I'm giving you the benefit of the doubt. I think the only people who saw you walk into the room were Jeremy and I. So I'm cutting you a big break. Don't disappoint me, Mike. No one screws with my best friend. Got that?"

****

"So how was the party?" Gina asked when I called later in the day.

"OK. Would have been better with you."

"That's what Sue said."

I coughed. My heart thumped. "What else did Sue say?"

"Nothing really. Said it was sort of boring. That I didn't miss anything."

I sighed. "Yeah. Sue's right. It wasn't one of Jeremy's better parties."

"Are you feeling better?" I asked.

"Yeah. Not one-hundred percent but a ton better than yesterday."

"Cool. Then we're on for tonight?" I asked.

"Yeah. Sue and Ron will meet us at the mall."

I sighed. "The mall? Really? I don't feel like shopping."

"We're not. I promise. Sue just wants to show me this bathing suit she's thinking about buying for senior week. Then we'll go to the movies like we had planned."

****

On the way to the mall, we stopped to get a burger. I was starving. I didn't have time after work to eat if I wanted to shower before I picked up Gina. Gina wasn't hungry, which was unusual. When we first started dating, she'd never order anything. I think she worried about me having enough money. It was kind of expensive. But the more we got to know one another, the more comfortable she became about eating in front of me. And man, can she eat. Sometimes more than me. I pay sometimes, and she pays sometimes. It depends on who has more money at the time. And if neither of us has money, which is often, we crash at Gina' s house and watch movies.

My luck Patty Monroe was the cashier. As soon as we walked up to the counter Patty threw her hair back and stuck out her chest. I couldn't look at her. I was so disgusted with myself. My heart beat like Led Zeppelin's John Bonham on the drums. I ordered the food while keeping my eyes on the menu boards overhead. Even when I went to pay for it, I placed the money on the counter without ever looking up at Patty.

"What was that all about?"Gina asked when we sat down.

"What?"

"You. You were acting weird. Like you didn't want to talk to Patty. I thought you were friends."

I coughed. "Friends? What made you think that?"

"Oh, I don't know," Gina said. "I know her parents and your parents are friends, so I figured you were friends."

"I'm not friends with Patty Monroe."

"Well, maybe she wants to be friends," Gina said.

I cleared my throat. "Maybe. I don't really know. Enough about Patty; I'd much rather talk about you."

I dipped a couple of fries in ketchup and popped them in my mouth. "Sure you don't want a fry?"

"Too greasy," Gina said. "I don't want to eat anything that'll upset my stomach. I don't want another night like last night."

Neither did I.

****

The food court was packed with high school kids, and the noise made my ears thump.

I leaned in to speak to Gina so she would be able to hear me. "See Sue anywhere?"

"We always sit across from the Chinese place," Gina said.

I followed Gina toward the opposite end of the food court.

"She's over there," Gina pointed. "Eating an egg roll."

We weaved through the crowd, having to shove one or two who were rude and refused to get out of the way. Sue didn't see us until we were practically on top of her table.

"It's about time you guys got here," Sue said. Sue flashed me a half smile and hugged Gina. They have been best friends since kindergarten. And if I ever doubted Sue's loyalty to Gina, last night and today took care of that.

41

"You guys want to wait here while I show Gina the suit?" Sue asked.

"Great idea," Ron said. "Although I wouldn't mind seeing you model it."

Sue hit Ron's arm playfully. "You'll see it – eventually." She winked her eyebrows. "Be back in a jiff."

Ron and I talked baseball while the girls shopped. Even though he didn't play for his school team, he liked watching games. His favorite team was the Red Sox and I loved the Yankees.

We went from talking baseball to talking about senior week at the beach.

"Are you going?" he asked.

"I plan on it. Been trying to save money. How about you?"

Ron shook his head. "Can't. Cost too much, and I gotta start work right after school's out to make some money for college. But can you do me a favor?"

"Sure."

"Keep an eye on Sue at the beach. I don't want any guys hitting on her, trying to pick her up. Not that I think she would go with them, but just don't want to give them a chance, you know? She can get a little loose when she drinks."

"No problem. I'll look out for her," I said. But I knew he didn't have anything to worry about. Sue was not only a faithful friend, but also a faithful girlfriend. Of that, I was certain.

****

When Gina and Sue returned, Sue held up a plastic shopping bag about the size of a sandwich bag. "Got it," she said.

"You got an entire swimsuit inside that bag?" I asked.

Sue winked at Ron. "Doesn't need to cover much."

Ron snatched the bag and peeked inside. "You can model it for me later. I have to approve, you know."

Sue grabbed the bag back. "Yeah, right."

"It can't be too sexy," Ron said. "Don't want other guys eyeing up what's mine."

"You have nothing to worry about," said Sue, kissing Ron on the cheek. "I would never cheat on you."

I squirmed in my seat. I knew Sue's comment was directed at me. She was never going to let me forget what a creep I had been. And I would never forget how she saved my ass and prevented me from making one of the biggest mistakes of my life.

There was an awkward pause before I suggested we head to the movie theater across from the mall. I was looking forward to the movie. Normally I'm not a big fan of romantic comedies, but Gina likes them, and I was hoping that the movie might get her in the mood to make out afterward.

Chapter 5

Mike

I couldn't wait to tell Gina about my day. I was with my parents at Madison, my dad's alma mater. I had visited before, but now that I knew for sure I'd be playing ball there on a baseball scholarship, it felt different.

I got to meet the other recruits along with the rest of the team. I got to see the dorm where the baseball players lived and learned about some of the other cool perks we got. Like being able to register for classes first and being able to study in a special room at the library if we wanted to.

The only bad part of going to Madison is that I would be so far away from Gina. She had decided on Theodore, a small private university on the other side of the state. We wouldn't be able to see each other that much. Probably only at holidays. Gina had been looking at Madison, too, but in the end decided that Theodore was a better fit. Theodore was in a more rural setting and the class sizes were small. Unlike the hundreds in a lecture hall at Madison, general elective classes at Theodore had no more than 40 people.

"So how was it?" Gina asked when I called.

"Great. The baseball facilities are top-notch."

"How about the dorms?"

"Better than I thought they'd be. There are built-in desks with shelves and closets with lots of storage space. A little small, but it's not like I'll be spending a lot of time in it anyhow. Probably just sleep there. What sucks is that we'll be so far apart."

"I know," Gina said. "But we can call each other and we'll see each other when we're home on breaks."

"But it's not going to be the same."

Gina changed the subject. She had been doing that a lot lately. And I was beginning to think that maybe going to different colleges was a good thing. I knew deep in my heart that Gina loved me, but the divide that had started in the early spring was growing wider. To be honest, I was not only frustrated but also mad that Gina didn't do more to stop our relationship from falling apart. I felt like I was the one trying to hold it together, and I was tired of being patient and understanding. I wanted to hold Gina, to make love to her and make her feel the way I used to make her feel. But she wouldn't let me, and it was killing me.

"Are we still on for tonight?" she asked.

"Absolutely. Seven sound good?"

"Perfect."

"Mind if we stop by the mall? I want to pick Coach up a card, thanking him for all he's done for me this season."

There was silence.

"Gina, are you there?"

"Yeah. Sorry. I heard you. That's fine. We can stop by the mall."

I hated picking out cards. There were too many to choose from. And after awhile they all read the same. But I wanted to find a thank-you card that said exactly what I felt. After all, Coach did a lot for me, and I wanted to let him know how much I appreciated it. I held up a blue card. "What do you think of this one?" I moved it toward Gina so she would take it.

She held up her hand. "That's OK. Whichever one you pick I'm sure is fine."

I pulled the card back. "What's with you?"

"Nothing. I just don't think I need to read the card."

"But I'd like your opinion."

Gina sighed and took the card and read it. "It's good."

"Do you like it better than this one?" I handed her another card I had pulled from the rack.

Gina sighed and grabbed the card from my hand. Her eyes quickly scanned the front and inside. "Either one is fine."

You would have thought I had asked Gina to do something horrible. All I wanted was for her to read a card I was buying for Coach. She should be happy that Coach did so much for me. I know she was happy that I got into Madison on a full ride. And since Coach played a huge part in that I would have thought she would be grateful to him.

"I guess it's this one then." I put the gray one back and took the blue one to the cashier.

****

Gina

I couldn't believe Mike wanted me to read the stupid thank-you card he was buying for Smith. He kept saying how great he was and how if it hadn't been for Smith he wouldn't have gotten into Madison. Wrong. If it hadn't been for me, Smith wouldn't have worked his ass off to get Mike into Madison. And if Mike wasn't so good, it wouldn't have mattered how hard Smith worked. Mike was giving Smith all of the credit and the truth was, while Smith might have helped because he had to, Mike was the one with the arm.

I wanted to tell the world what Smith had done. It killed me that Mike thought he was such a great person when I knew the truth. Mike had put the bastard on a pedestal and I wanted to knock him the hell off. But if keeping silent meant Mike was getting what he wanted, than that was the price I had to pay.

I kept thinking about Pastor Greg's wilderness sermon, and I wondered how long I'd be in this wilderness. I just couldn't see through the dense underbrush and thicket to find my way out. Each time I thought I found a bit of a clearing, trees would fall around me, blocking my path and causing me to sink deeper in the mire. It was like those dreams I used to have as a child where I was running away from a monster but no matter how fast my legs moved I didn't go anywhere.

It occurred to me that I could report the rape after baseball season was over. Smith couldn't take it out on Mike. But what proof did I have? Again, none. It would be his word against mine.

I knew that Mike was getting frustrated with me. We hadn't gone the whole way in weeks. I wanted to, I really did. But every time I thought I was going to be OK, I'd freeze. I'd see Smith's bushy brows and bald head and smell his nasty beer breath. And that damn dime-size mole between his belly button and pubic hair.

I know that I really freaked out Mike the night I flipped out. He playfully placed my hand on his crotch and it sent me into a sobbing rage. I kept thinking about Smith and how he forced my hand on his bulging crotch and said that his was bigger than Mike's and how much I would like it. Poor Mike, about all he could do was hold me. And the worst part was that he knew something was really wrong and that I wasn't sharing it with him. I've always told Mike everything. There have never been any secrets between us – until now.

Before the crotch incident and me melting into a puddle of tears, Mike asked if I was pregnant. I had wished out loud that I was. Being pregnant with Mike's child would be so much easier to deal with. The timing would be all wrong, but at least it's something I want to happen – eventually.

I was mad at myself, too, for not getting over what happened quicker. I know I can't be the only person who's gone through this. Normally when bad stuff happens, I can shake it off. But I couldn't shake this off, and that made me mad.

We were on our way out of the card store when we ran into Julie hanging on a guy neither of us knew. Julie went to our school but the guy looked older. Julie went through boyfriends like I went through packs of orange sugarless gum. She was tall and tan and lean and it seemed like guys were always tripping over her.

"What number is that?" Mike whispered as we walked away. He was referring to the guy Julie was with.

"I've stopped counting," I said.

Just a few days before, I had found Julie crying in the bathroom at school. Black mascara stained her cheeks and her hair was a mess, like she had been pulling it in every direction.

"Julie, what's wrong?" I asked.

"Everything," she said. "My life sucks. I'm tired of being used."

I put my arm around her and she fell into my shoulder. "Then stop."

She pulled back and looked at me with swollen raccoon eyes. "You just don't get it. I'm not like you. Smart and all."

"Don't say that," I said. "You just have to work a little harder. And I can help."

The next day I saw her with a new guy. And now today, with yet another one. I knew she wouldn't call me for homework help as sure as I knew that this new guy wouldn't last.

I knew that Julie was in her own wilderness and that she was going to have to find her way out just like I was going to have to find the way out of mine. It made me realize that you never know what someone might be going through, you never know what their wilderness stories are or if they're stuck in one. We each have crosses to bear, I suppose. The trick is not to get weighed down by them.

We were the last couple to arrive at Jeremy's house. Unlike Jeremy's usual parties, this one was just for couples. His parents liked to travel and were never home so we always had a place to hang out. It was me and Mike, Sue and Ron, Jeremy and Ellen, Becky and Bill and Amy (aka Cookie) and Keith. Dave wanted to bring the ninth-grader he was seeing but Jeremy told him that he better hadn't because the rest of us would kill him. We were still all sore that he broke up with Diane right before our senior prom.

Jeremy got his older cousin to get us a couple of cases. It felt good to just hang out with everyone. I knew we wouldn't have many more moments like this. In two weeks, we would be graduating and everyone would be going their own way. Becky would be leaving for basic training in the Air Force and the rest of us would head off to college.

I tasted the homemade salsa Ellen made. She was a terrific cook and was excited about culinary school. "This is so good, El. I especially love the chopped avocados."

"You know what they say about avocados," Becky said. "They're an aphrodisiac."

Ron dipped a chip into the salsa and held it up to Sue's mouth. "In that case, eat a lot of it."

"I don't think she'll need that," Jeremy said. "Just give her another beer."

Jeremy's remark made Sue cough and she spit the salsa all over Ron.

"That works, too," said Ron, wiping the salsa off his shirt. "And maybe it's not quite as messy as the salsa."

Everyone laughed.

"Do you know that the Aztecs called the avocado tree "testicle tree?" Becky asked.

"How do they get testicle out of an avocado?" Jeremy asked.

"They thought that a pair of avocados hanging together on a tree looked like a pair of testicles."

Jeremy scrunched his nose. "I will never look at an avocado the same way again."

"You eat bananas, right?" Becky asked.

"Yeah, so."

"That's another aphrodisiac," Becky said. "The shape alone is sexual."

I squirmed in my seat. All of the aphrodisiac talk was making me a little uncomfortable. And the more beer that my friends drank the looser they became. After awhile, there were only a few couples in the room; the rest had left to make out.

Cookie pulled the tab on another Miller Lite. "Have you seen Karen lately? She's getting big. She's not supposed to have the baby until the end of June, but she told me the other day that she could go early."

Karen was our classmate. She got pregnant to an older guy. She claimed she was on the pill and got pregnant anyhow. She was planning a fall wedding, and said she didn't want to look like a white elephant waddling down the aisle.

"But she looks good," I said. "And you know Karen, with all the sports she plays she'll have it off in no time."

I thought for sure that Karen would go to college and become a gym teacher. She was the best female athlete in our school and lettered in track, basketball and field hockey. It sucked that she got pregnant especially if she was on the pill. I couldn't imagine how I would feel if I would have gotten pregnant after what Smith did to me. Carrying his kid would have been horrible.

I looked at Cookie and Keith, kissing on the couch. Keith was the first boy I ever kissed. We were in sixth grade and playing Spin the Bottle in Becky's garage. I spun the empty beer bottle, and when it stopped, it was pointing at Keith.

I wasn't sure if I was supposed to open my mouth when we kissed. The girls and I had talked about it but I realized we hadn't made a decision. My heart felt like it was going to pop out of my chest. I wiggled over to Keith and I leaned in and he leaned in and we kissed. It was as quick as a firefly's light.

Funny the memories that come rushing back at odd times. But being at Jeremy's, hanging with my friends, knowing that graduation was only a couple of weeks away, made me retrospective.

Mike leaned over and whispered in my ear. "Wanna get out of here? Go to the woods?"

I nodded. I was going to try to be the old me, but I didn't want to do it at Jeremy's house. I wanted to be alone with Mike under our tree in our woods. That's where I wanted to be, more than anything. And I hoped that I could relax enough to let down my guard and let the one person I loved more than anything in.

Chapter 6

Gina

The woods where we made out were part of Mike's uncle's farm. His uncle Jim cut a road into the woods so he could easily access the trees when he needed to cut firewood. Mike said it was a safe place to make out because no one, except his uncle, ever used the road. And Uncle Jim wouldn't be using it at night.

I'm pretty sure Mike told him that we went there, just in case he ever saw car lights going down the lane.

We passed the lane going back to the farm and shortly after turned down the dirt road leading into the woods. I bounced as we navigated the bumps and potholes.

Mike glanced over at me. "Feeling OK?"

I smiled. "Yeah. Just thinking about graduation. That reminds me. Mom wants to have my graduation party on the Saturday after we graduate but I told her I wanted to check to see when you're having yours."

"Mine's on Friday night," Mike said. "Everyone's supposed to come back to the house afterward. So it looks like that will all work out."

Mike turned off the car. "There's a lot of stars out tonight. I bet we can find the Big Dipper."

I smiled because I remembered what one of my best friends, J.R., had told me.

"Did you know that the Big Dipper and the Little Dipper aren't constellations but asterisms?"

Mike shook his head.

"J.R. told me that."

Mike wasn't fond of J.R., mostly because he knew how J.R. felt about me. J.R. was in love with me and had been for a long time. I never had any romantic feelings for J.R. He was the brother I never had. Mike knew this but it didn't stop him from being jealous.

Mike stared straight ahead. "I read what J.R. wrote in your yearbook."

I reached over and touched his hand. "When?"

He turned and looked at me. "You gave it to me to sign after he had signed it. I didn't go looking for it. But it was hard not to miss. It took up half a page."

"We're just friends," I said.

"But he'd like to be more," Mike chimed in. "And he said something about an incident. What's that all about?"

I wasn't about to tell Mike that J.R. tried to kiss me one night while we were playing pool at his house. He backed off as soon as I turned away. J.R. apologized over and over and I told him to just forget it. I was OK. Everything was cool.

"Come on, Mike," I said. "I don't know what incident J.R. was referring to, and I'd much rather talk about us."

"You're right," Mike said. "I'm sorry I even brought it up. Let's find our tree."

We walked hand-in-hand into the woods and found our tree. I ran my hands over the words we had carved in the rough bark. "Mike and Gina forever." I smiled. I'll always remember that night. It was the first time we told each other that we loved one another. Mike wanted to record it for all eternity. So he dug out the pocketknife he had gotten in Scouts and carved our names, enclosing them in a heart.

"It's never going away," said Mike, unzipping the blue sleeping bag. "Just like I'm never going away."

Mike spread the sleeping bag out with the plaid liner facing up. He grabbed his T-shirt at his shoulders and pulled it over his head. There was just enough moonlight to see the ring of thorns that wrapped around his right bicep.

"Looks like the weight lifting is paying off," I said, reaching out to touch his tattoo.

Mike sat down on the sleeping bag and held out his arm. "Come here."

I sat down beside him. He brushed my hair off my face. "You're so beautiful."

I closed my eyes as he outlined my lips with his thumb. I opened my mouth and his finger slipped inside and I playfully bite it and circled it with the tip of my tongue.

I tried to focus on Mike, his gorgeous, thick curls and beautiful smile. I ran my fingers through his hair and I heard him moan softly. I played with his ear and let my fingers trail down to his lips. I rubbed my fingers over his lips and down to his chin before I pulled his head toward me and found his soft lips. Playful kisses led to deep kisses and I felt the familiar tingle I hadn't felt since before the rape. So far, so good. I rubbed my hand over Mike's chest and down his arms. He slid his hands under my shirt, unhooked my bra and slipped my shirt over my head. We hugged bare chest against bare chest. He was warm and it felt good being next to his skin. I reached down to unzip his jeans.

"I'll take care of this," he said, and wiggled off his jeans and boxers. I saw his boxers in the moonlight and it sent me reeling back to the rape. His boxers were the same blue boxers Smith had worn. I could see the Fruit of the Loom tag.

I was squirming on the cold vinyl floor. Tears flooded my face. The gag hurt my mouth. I felt the panic. I couldn't breathe. I wanted to escape but I didn't know how. I could smell Coach Smith, the beer and stale smoke. I could feel him tearing me apart inside. It hurt. I could hear his skin slapping mine as he rammed into me and told me how much I liked what he was doing. I watched his hips move back and forth as he violated me.

Heavy sobs wracked my body and Mike held me in his arms. "It's OK, Gina, baby. Everything's OK. You're safe. I'm not going to hurt you. No one's going to hurt you."

Mike got dressed and dressed me and kissed me on the forehead and we laid there on the sleeping bag under our tree.

"Gina," Mike whispered after awhile. "It's OK. We don't have to try that again. I'm all right just laying here beside you and holding you."

I'm not sure when I stopped sobbing that night. I cried for what I had lost. I cried because I felt that I would never be the same person I was before it all happened. Mostly, I cried because I realized that it was only a matter of time before I was going to leave Mike. He deserved better than what I was able to give him. I couldn't be the girl he wanted me to be. That girl was gone.

Maybe forever.

****

Mike

I'm not sure what happened. Everything was going great. Gina seemed relaxed. I was letting her lead. I didn't want to move too fast and then turn her off. After she unzipped my jeans, I took them off. That's when Gina freaked. It was like Jekyll and Hyde. One minute she was all into it and the next minute she wasn't.

I've never seen Gina act this way. Watching her was like watching a runaway train. It just keeps going and you feel so helpless because you know it's going to crash and there's not a damn thing you can do to stop it. And it's the crash that I was worried about. How bad will it be? The casualty count? About all I could do was hold Gina and let her sob.

I was beginning to wonder, though, if something sexual happened to Gina that she couldn't talk about. There had to be some reason why she froze every time we got past kissing and touching. It's about the only thing that made sense. Maybe something happened with J.R. I knew they played tennis a lot and they didn't seem to play as much lately.

I knew that Gina thought of J.R. as a brother but that he loved her and would like nothing more than for Gina to see him the way he saw her. No. It couldn't be that. As much as I disliked J.R. I know that he would never hurt Gina. He cares too much about her.

I just couldn't quite figure out what had happened, but I was beginning to see that if I loved Gina, I was going to have to let her go. I didn't want to pressure her or make her feel crappy every time we tried to make out. I needed to let her go so she could figure out whatever the hell was going on.

What'd she call it? Yeah, her wilderness. I needed to let her find the way out of her wilderness. I was pissed that she wasn't letting me help her, but there was a part of me that knew that maybe Gina was right. She needed to do this alone. And I definitely didn't want to make it more complicated and difficult than it already was.

****

Gina

It was a few weeks after graduation. The parties were over and senior week was history. Mom and Dad were out with friends and Mike came over to watch movies.

Mike sat on the couch beside me. He took my hands in his and kissed each one. "You just don't seem to trust me, Gina. I've tried. I've really tried. I've been patient and I've tried not to push you. I didn't even pressure you into having sex during senior week, which, by the way, was incredibly hard. Everyone else was screwing but us. But it's not just the sex I miss. I miss you. The Gina I loved before this new Gina came into the picture. Sometimes I feel like I don't even know you anymore. You and I know that we can't go on like this. I love you. I'll always love you. But, what's that you called it? Wilderness? You need to get out of that wilderness you're in."

Tears pooled in my eyes. Mike was right. I did have trust issues. I couldn't trust anyone anymore – even him. After all, I had kind-of, sort-of trusted Smith and he betrayed that trust.

I bit my bottom lip and the tears came without being called. Mike handed me the box of tissues on the end table. I blew my nose and nodded. "You're right."

Mike sighed. "You've also become more and more withdrawn. You don't want to go out much anymore, and you never tell me anything."

I grabbed a throw pillow and hugged it. "You're right. I need to get my head on straight. I'm sorry. This just isn't working. I'm screwed up. I've been screwed up for awhile. I need to get unscrewed because I definitely don't want to screw you up, too."

Mike bolted up. "I didn't mean that I wanted to break up, just that things have to change."

"Things aren't going to change until I change. And I'm not going to change because I can't change. At least I haven't been able to yet. I think it's time that we break up. You deserve more than I can give you now. I'm sorry."

Mike jumped off the couch and threw his arms in the air. "I can't believe you're throwing everything we had away. Just like that." He snapped his fingers. "That it didn't mean anything to you."

I stood up. "That's not fair. It means everything to me. That's why I'm doing what I'm doing."

Mike grabbed my shoulders and his eyes bore into mine. "Gina, baby. Do you realize how incredibly stupid that sounds?"

"But it's the truth. I need to work through some stuff."

Mike threw his arms in the air again. "Yeah, stuff that you refuse to tell me about."

I crossed my arms. "Right, stuff that's mine and mine alone to work out. But it's not that I don't love you."

"Yeah, right."

"Mike, I have always loved you and I always will. But sometimes loving someone means letting them go."

Mike punched the air. "Fuck that, Gina. That's a line of crap. When you love someone you trust them, you don't keep things from them. When you love someone you want to spend the rest of your life with them. Not throw everything away that you worked so hard to build."

"Fine. Then I don't love you anymore," I said.

As soon as I said it, I knew it was the answer. It was the only way. I think a part of me always knew it would come to this. My heart felt like glass being shattered into millions of pieces, and I knew that it would never be the same, that no matter how hard I'd try to put those pieces back together there would always be lost slivers.

"Look me in the eyes and tell me that," Mike demanded. He grabbed me by the shoulders again and I looked into his eyes and watched as a deluge poured out of them and soaked his cheeks.

I swallowed hard. The only way this was going to work, that Mike was going to leave, was if he believed what I was telling him. And the only way to make him believe what I was telling him was to tell him a lie so good that I believed it myself. It would be the biggest lie that I ever told, but I would do it if it meant saving him. It was also a lie I had been practicing, knowing deep down that this day was near.

I took a deep breath and steadied myself, looking Mike right in his eyes. "Mike, I'm sorry. I just don't love you anymore. I haven't for quite awhile. I've been pretending because I didn't want to hurt you. But the truth is it was over for me a long time ago."

Mike shook his head. "You're lying. Come on, Gina. You've got to do better than that."

"It's true," I said. "I feel like I've been an actress in a play. I've been playing this part because I didn't want to hurt you. The truth is I can't play the part anymore. I wish I would have had the courage to tell you before this. I've felt like this for months and just didn't want to hurt you, so I kept it to myself, hoping that I would change my mind or somehow those old feelings would resurface. But they haven't. I care about you, but not enough to keep what we had going. I want more. I want someone different. I'm so sorry. I never meant to hurt you. I wish I could change everything and that you would be happy. But I can't. No more pretending."

Mike shook his head like he couldn't believe his ears. Tears exploded from his dark eyes and his face turned tomato red. He grabbed his hair and pulled it and kicked the hassock and walked out the door.

And he never looked back.

The door slammed behind him and I ran to my room and threw myself on my bed, soaking my Snow White quilt with my tears.

I felt horrible and worthless and mean. All of the negative verbs in the dictionary would not be enough to describe how I felt. But I knew that the only way to get Mike to go was to lie about how I really felt. And I knew that I played the part well. That he believed every word I said, and he hated me for it.

But I hated myself more.

Chapter 7

20 Years Later

Mike

The line to get into the funeral home wrapped around the brick three-story building on Main Street. I wondered if I would see anyone that I went to high school with. I knew Jeremy was coming, but I wasn't sure about any of the others. I felt a hand on my back and I turned around. It was Cookie. Despite living in nearby towns, I hadn't seen her since graduation.

"Michael Parker. How the hell have you been?"

She hugged me before I could even get my arms up.

"I've been good; great actually. Read about you in the paper."

Cookie smiled so wide her eyes winked. "Well, you know me."

I laughed. Cookie hadn't changed. She was a giant of a girl and still looked like she could whip my ass and knock me out cold in seconds. She was one tough lady. She's the only girl I know who could palm a basketball. "You always did stand up for what you believed in," I told her.

The newspaper article was about her school district banning books because they had bad words and contained too much violence. I think the official wording was "sexually explicit content, offensive language, and violence." Cookie led the opposition. I always thought she should have been a teen during the 60s. I could see her protesting the Vietnam War and listening to Bob Dylan, Janis Joplin and Joan Baez.

"How old is your son?" Cookie asked.

"Jack's ten."

"Does he play baseball like his old man?"

I laughed. "Yeah, and he's a lot better than I was at his age. Playing baseball is all he wants to do. What about you? Any kids? "

Cookie rolled her eyes. "Two girls. They're twins."

"Oh, no. Double trouble, huh?"

"You can say that. They're teenagers and the shit they wear to school drives me freakin' mad. The guys gotta have constant hard-ons. Zara was sent home from school the other day because her ass was sticking out of her skirt. Of course, I told her that would happen but did she listen to me? Noooo. Mom's never right. "

We laughed.

"Just be glad you don't have a girl," Cookie said.

"Sounds like they take after their mother," I told her.

Cookie playfully hit me on the arm. "What's that supposed to mean? I never dressed like a whore working the Boulevard."

"True. But you did dress differently and you never cared what anyone thought. It's one of the things I liked about you. You always did your own thing. Remember the time you wore three sets of leg warmers and that oversized sweatshirt that came down to the middle of your thigh?"

Cookie laughed. "I remember. My legs were so hot that day! I felt like a damn bear in heat."

I scanned her ivory silk blouse and black pants. "Now look at you. The typical suburban mom."

Cookie chuckled. "Sooner or later, we all end up there, I guess."

I turned around and realized there was a gap between me and the person in front of me. I closed the gap, with Cookie following on my heels.

"Whatever happened to that guy you went out with after you broke up with Keith?" I asked.

"You mean Bill. We didn't even last a month. He wanted to be able to date other girls in college. He kissed like a damn frog anyhow. Too much lick. Always felt like a damn fly. The last I heard he was working as an engineer for some oil company in Texas."

Cookie was killing me. I felt like an asshole laughing while standing in line to see a dead man. I thought that maybe we should switch to a more somber topic, given the occasion and all. "Shame about Doug dying. Every time I drive past where it happened I think of him."

"Yeah, me, too," Cookie said. "He was the first one in our class to die. Not sure about any others. Guess we'll find out at the reunion. Are you going?"

I grimaced. "Man, I don't know. I haven't been to any yet."

"This is the 20th; you should come. Bring your wife."

Guess Cookie hadn't heard about the divorce. "We're not together anymore."

Cookie's hand flew to her mouth. "Damn! Sorry, Mike. Me and my big mouth. I didn't know or I wouldn't have gone on like that."

"It's OK. We're friends. It wasn't one of those divorces where people end up hating each other. Just didn't work out."

"So do you have joint custody of Jack?" Cookie asked.

I nodded. "And we live close so Jack can come and go as he pleases no matter which house he's sleeping at. He has a baby sister so he seems to be at my house more lately. I don't think he likes the crying."

Cookie popped a mint in her mouth. "That's cool that you and your ex are friends. That has to be great for Jack. I don't know of any divorced couples who ended up on good terms. Most of the ones I know would kill each other if they had the chance, including me. The only thing good about the loser I was married to was that he stopped being able to get it up because of his health. Suited me just fine because he was a lousy lay anyway. Mr. Vibrator did a better job than he ever did. When Hubs No. 2 came along, didn't need the vibrator anymore." She laughed.

One thing about Cookie, you always knew what she thought. The woman definitely didn't hold anything back.

"Yeah, Lisa and I just realized a little too late that that's all we really were – friends. She deserved someone who could love her in the way she deserved to be loved. I wasn't that guy. But her husband, Jack's step-dad, is a good guy. A dentist. I'm happy for her."

I looked around as we turned the corner; the door was about thirty feet away. "Anyone else coming?"

"Sue and Diane said they were going to stop by, and I saw Keith and Tom leaving as I pulled into the parking lot."

"Do you see the old gang much?" I asked.

"Not really," Cookie said. "My kids had Diane for county honors band and I run into Sue from time to time. What about you?"

"I see Jeremy. And sometimes Tom."

Cookie smiled. "Some things never change.

"But that's about it. Ever hear from Gina?" I asked. Twenty years have passed and my heart still races when I say her name.

Cookie shook her head. "I know Sue does. Gina is Chloe's godmother. She's not married, I know that. And she's a killer prosecutor, according to Sue."

"A prosecutor? I always thought she'd be a writer."

"She works in the sex crimes/child abuse bureau," Cookie said. "Prosecutes rape crimes. Sue said she works all the time. Sue's trying to convince her to come to the reunion. Says she's thinking about it."

Gina wasn't married. She was a prosecutor. Damn, I had no idea. I wanted to know more, but I didn't want to seem overly interested.

"Think a lot of people will come to this one, since it's the big 2-0?" I asked.

Cookie shrugged her shoulders. "I don't know. I hope so. Maybe at this one people will be over having to prove that they've made it. At the other ones, there was a lot of that. 'Oh, I did this and that.' Really? Who cares? Cause I didn't come to the reunion to hear you brag about all the great stuff you've done since high school," Cookie said.

"Yeah, I know what you mean."

We were finally at the door. I whispered to Cookie, "It was great seeing you. And I'll think about the reunion. I still have the invitation at home."

I made my way through the crowd to where Coach Smith's wife and sons stood by the casket. The boys towered over their mom. They were well over six feet, dressed in black suits and white shirts. Their mom, wearing a short black dress, looked more like their sister.

I shook their hands and expressed my condolences. Mrs. Smith remembered me.

"Thanks for coming," she said. "Rich would be honored that so many of his former players came."

I walked by his mahogany casket, topped with dozens of red roses. I sneezed. Flowers always made me sneeze. The red roses reminded me of Gina. I had saved money for weeks to get her a dozen red roses for our first Valentine's Day. I worked at the grocery store stocking shelves so it's not like I was raking in the greens. I can still see Gina's smile when she opened the door and I handed her the long white box tied with a red ribbon. Gina loved roses and said that she wanted to carry a bouquet of red roses when we got married.

I couldn't wait to get outside, away from all of the people. I wasn't much for crowds, and I hated waiting in lines. It's one of the reasons I didn't like taking Jack to the amusement park. Those lines were ridiculous. My head pounded as I weaved through the parking lot to my car.

I couldn't stop thinking about Gina not being married. It's all I thought about on the drive home. That and what I had learned about her prosecuting sex crimes. How did I not know that?

It was Lisa's night to have Jack, so I came home to an empty house. I threw a turkey and cheese sandwich together and grabbed the reunion invitation off the desk in the den.

The invitation wasn't fancy. It was a piece of white computer paper folded in thirds. I couldn't stop thinking about Gina, wondering if she would come. After our breakup, I tried reaching out to her but she would never take my calls or return my letters. Finally, I stopped trying. I couldn't take the rejection anymore. But I always wondered about that wilderness stuff Gina had talked about. Did she ever make it out?

When I met Lisa a couple years later, I thought that I was over Gina, but I don't think I've ever gotten over her. Before dating Lisa, I found myself trying to find someone who looked like Gina. It's not easy finding girls who have long red hair. After awhile, I realized that I was trying to replace what I had lost and that wasn't cool. I needed to move on. And I thought I had when Lisa came into my life. She wasn't anything like Gina. Gina was tall with gorgeous legs that went on forever. Lisa was much shorter and had blond hair. She was a Tasmanian devil on the basketball court and could beat me in the mile without even trying.

Don't get me wrong. What Lisa and I had was great. But there was just something that wasn't there on my part. Lisa sensed it from the very beginning but convinced herself that it didn't matter, that she loved me enough for both of us. When she told me this it broke my heart. I never meant to hurt her, and I really wished that I could have felt the way about her that she felt about me. We agreed that Jack was the best of both of us and that for his sake, we'd be friends. Lisa's happy and I'm happy that she's happy.

I get lonely sometimes and I've dated some, but there's no one special in my life. There's a woman I work with that I sometimes hook up with. It's convenient and she doesn't want any commitment so it works. But it's just sex. That's all. And it always leaves me feeling like there has to be more.

****

Gina

Even though Sue's my best friend, I never told her that Smith raped me. There were so many times that I wanted to, but I just couldn't bring myself to do it. The only person I told was the therapist who helped me deal with the flashbacks and pain long after that brutal night. So when Sue went on and on about the funeral when she called, it was hard for me to listen. I hated the bastard. I was glad he was dead.

"The line was out the building and around the corner," Sue said. "I figured there would be a crowd, but it was way more people than I had expected. Coach Smith must have touched a lot of lives. "

I coughed. *And ruined some*, I thought. I picked up the magazine that had come in the mail that day and thumbed through it while I listened.

"And they had this slideshow with photos of him and his family over the years that played continuously, and his baseball uniform and glove and some other stuff was scattered on tables throughout the room."

I gritted my teeth. "That's nice."

"I felt so bad for his wife and sons. They looked pretty whipped," Sue said.

"I'm sure."

"Are you listening to me, Gina?"

How did she know I was looking at my magazine? "Of course, why?

"Well, it doesn't seem like you're saying much," Sue said.

"I'm listening. You said his wife and sons looked pretty whipped. See? I'm listening."

I could hear Sue sigh through my earpiece.

"You never liked him much, did you?" Sue asked.

I could feel my muscles tense up, especially my neck and shoulders. I had spent the last twenty years dealing with what the creep did to me. No, I hated the son of a bitch.

"He was OK," I told Sue.

"Remember our calc final? It was so hard. You were the only one in the entire class who got an A, which totally amazed me because I was doing better than you were in the class."

I silently snickered. If only Sue knew why I got the A.

"Oh, almost forgot. Mike was at Smith's funeral. Chloe and I ran into Cookie and her two girls at the mall. She waited in line with Mike."

Hearing Mike and Smith mentioned in the same sentence made my heart race. Then I realized I was holding my breath and forced myself to breathe.

"Oh, yeah?" I said. "Mike was there?"

"Yeah. Did you know he's divorced?"

I spit the hot tea I had just taken a sip of all over the fashion spread in the magazine. I had no idea Mike and Lisa got a divorce. The last I heard they had a son and were happy. "No, I didn't know that."

"Yeah. Apparently his ex remarried a couple of years ago and has a daughter that's about one. Mike told Cookie that they're still friends. They just realized too late that that's all they ever really were."

I closed the magazine and tossed it aside. "I had no idea."

"Me, neither, but I thought you'd want to know."

"Now why would I want to know that Mike is divorced?" I asked.

"Oh, I don't know," Sue said. "Maybe because you've never stopped caring about him."

"Oh, come on, Sue. It's been twenty years."

"That's right. It has been. And in those twenty years you've never stopping loving him. You might be able to fool other people, but you can't fool me. God only knows why you broke it off in high school. I've never been able to figure that one out."

"I told you why. I didn't love him anymore."

"I know that's what you said, but it's a crock of shit," Sue said.

"It's not like I haven't dated other guys," I said. "I even had one propose to me."

"Sure, you've dated. But you've never married. Christ, you've never even lived with a guy. And spending weekends is not living with a guy, Gina. So that one guy, the one who asked you to marry him, doesn't count."

"Can we talk about something else?" I asked. "You haven't asked me about my doctor's appointment yet."

"OK. How did your doctor's appointment go?"

"Great. He gave me lots of information to look through. Each sperm donor is assigned a number. It's like looking through a catalog. There's tons of information, like eye and hair color, ethnicity, height and weight, blood type."

"So you're really going to go through with it?"

"You know how much I've always wanted a child. I'm 38. It's now or never. I can afford a nanny and Mom said she'll come down for several weeks afterward to help."

"And you know Chloe and I will help in any way we can."

"I know. And I appreciate that. It'll be like a sister for Chloe. "

"So, you decided on a girl?"

"I would love both, but I thought that if I'm going to be a single parent, that probably a girl is best. At least I know what to expect."

"Good point," Sue said. "Did you get the flier about the reunion?" Sue asked.

"Yeah. Got it and tossed it in the trash."

"Gina! Come on. Come home and go to this one. It's been 20 years. Everyone would love to see you."

I sighed.

"Promise me you'll think about it," Sue said. "You and I can go together. Like old times."

"OK. I'll think about it."

"Might see Mike there."

I had wondered if he would go. "Is he going?"

"Cookie told me that he was thinking about it. He hasn't committed yet. But you read those love stories all the time about high school sweethearts that reconnect at high school reunions."

"You've always been a hopeless romantic."

"But it could happen," Sue said.

"Could, but I think that stuff is more fairy tale than anything else. I'm not the same person I was in high school. You know that. And I'm sure Mike isn't either. Twenty years have passed and a lot has happened in those twenty years."

"Yeah, I've gotten fatter," Gina laughed.

"I'm serious. My life is so different than I ever would have imagined. I love what I do. I've worked hard to be one of the county's top prosecutors. I wouldn't give up my life for anyone. And now I'm going to become a mom and all of my energy and focus will go into being the best mom I can be. Yes, I would have preferred becoming a mom the traditional way, but life, as we both know, doesn't always turn out the way we always thought or wished it would."

When I got off the phone with Sue, I picked up the sperm donor profiles. I felt a little weird, like I was trying to put together a designer baby. I guess in a way I was. I wanted my child to look like me, so red hair was important.

Each profile came with notes from the interviewer.

Donor came to our interview wearing khakis (with one leg rolled up for bike riding), and a button-down shirt. His reddish hair is cut short. He has closely cut facial hair and perfectly straight, white teeth. He has light skin with some freckles. His hobbies include playing sports ….

I yawned. I had had enough for one night. I wished that I had someone who would just pick the perfect sperm for me. I was on information overload. I'd have to do an excel spreadsheet and rate each donor on various factors. Or maybe I should compose a rubric and then rate each donor that way. I'd go with the one with the highest composite score and in the event of a tie I'd have to consider secondary information, like the interviewer's notes.

Chapter 8

Mike

Seeing Cookie at Coach Smith's funeral sure made me think about things I hadn't thought about in a long time. Like the night Gina broke up with me. I still remember that night, as if it were an inning ago. Probably because it hit me so hard, like a batter who rips the cover off a ball. It nails you in the gut, knocks the wind out of you and forces your eyeballs into the infield as you blink the dirt, clay, sand and silt away. Damn, Gina. After all these years, I'm still blinking.

That night, sitting in Gina's living room, she looked me straight in the eyes and told me that she didn't love me anymore. She said she had been pretending. That it was over. Wow. Even thinking about it now makes me tense.

I just didn't get it. I didn't get how she could be so into me one minute and not the next. I always thought there was something else going on, especially because Gina had been acting so weird for weeks, but I could never figure it out.

After the breakup, I'd call Gina every so often just so I could hear her voice. As soon as she answered the phone I'd hang up.

I have to admit that when Cookie told me Gina wasn't married, it gave me a rush. Like maybe she never found anyone she loved more than she once loved me. Not that I'm egotistical, but Gina and I did have something pretty good. And hearing she was unattached made me wonder for a second if maybe we could hook up.

After Gina broke it off, I threw the sleeping bag we always used for making out in a dumpster behind the mall. I haven't been back to that spot in the woods since. I just never felt comfortable taking another girl there. The tree was our place. Our names were carved in it. It kind of scared me that just hearing Gina's name could trigger such strong feelings in me twenty years later.

There were so many things I had wondered about her. What was her husband like? How many kids did she have? Did they have red hair? Gina always wanted a girl with red hair. I never would have guessed Gina would become a prosecutor. I thought she always wanted to be a writer. It didn't surprise me, though, that she'd choose the sex crimes unit. She always fought for people who couldn't fight for themselves.

There was this guy, Ray, in our class. He was a little backward but he could draw like Picasso. Some of the guys made fun of him. If one of them made a comment about Ray when Gina was around, she'd lay into them. And there was a druggie, Joe who Gina befriended. She saw something good in him when no one else did. He ended up in rehab and now counsels drug addicts.

About the only person Gina wasn't fond of was Peter. He creeped her out because he always stared at her. It weirded her out so much that I talked to Peter about it. I think I made him piss his pants when I cornered him in the locker room. I wasn't going to hurt him; I just wanted him to stop looking at my girl. After that, Gina didn't complain about him anymore.

Damn. I hadn't thought about all these people in years.

I hated the house when Jack was at Lisa's. It was too quiet. I walked into his room and sat on his bed. It reminded me of my room when I was his age – junk everywhere. Comic books stacked on his nightstand. His baseball glove, spikes and bat scattered on the floor. Comic hero posters taped to the walls and clothing hung half out of his dresser drawers. He definitely preferred things messy.

The phone rang. It was Jack. He was calling to say goodnight. It was something Lisa started. She thought it was important for Jack to tell me goodnight on the nights he wasn't with me. And, of course, when he slept at my house, I made sure he called her.

I picked up the black-framed photo of me and Jack sitting on his computer desk. We were making funny faces. Jack was about four at the time. Looking at him, you'd never guess he was my kid. He has blond hair and fair skin like his mom. Side by side, we looked like an Oreo with a missing wafer.

****

Gina

I dug the reunion invitation out of the trash. The reunion was six weeks away. I wondered how much weight I could lose in six weeks. If I went to the reunion, I wanted to look good. Not just average, but good. I've always exercised and never had to worry about eating cakes and cookies and the salty snacks I loved. But my body was changing, and I couldn't eat all the junk I used to eat and stay a size 8, even with the exercising. It was a bitch getting older.

I remember when I was in high school and we celebrated Mom's fortieth birthday. I remember thinking how old that was. Now that I'm almost forty, it seems so young. I don't feel old. Even the fertility doctor said lots of women are waiting to have children until their late 30s or early 40s.

Although he said some have to use donor eggs because their eggs are not viable.

I sipped my tea as I checked my calendar to see if I would be out of town for work the day of the reunion. Turned out I was in Atlanta the week before and Chicago two weeks later. But that week was free.

I stood naked in front of the full-length mirror mounted on the back of my bathroom door. I rubbed my hand over my stomach then pinched my belly fat. I doubted that I could lose two inches in six weeks. It wasn't like when I was a teenager and could exist on water and crackers for a few days to drop some weight before the prom. I long since gave up the cracker and water diet, but running consistently might help. It did seem silly, though, trying to get a flat stomach when I was going to turn around and get pregnant.

I turned sideways, wondering what that view would look like when I was nine months pregnant. Sue said that she got so big that her belly button turned inside out. It was the only time that her belly button was free of dirt and dust, she said. Now, she uses Q-tips and tweezers to clean the creases like the rest of us.

I can't imagine my stomach being that big. And yet, the thought comforts me. I feel powerful. Just the idea of a baby growing inside of me makes my head spin. I want to feel a baby kick inside of me. Now, at this point in my life, there's nothing I want more.

I sometimes wonder what I will tell my daughter when she asks me about her daddy. Do I tell her the truth? That he was just a number on a sheet of paper that I picked because he was smart and good looking? That I shopped for her like I would a designer dress? It feels so wrong in so many ways, but I don't exactly have a choice. I'm cognizant that time is my enemy and the longer I wait, the more difficult it will be.

It's weird when I think about something how it seems to turn up everywhere. Like now that I've decided to have a baby, I see babies everywhere. I page through a magazine and see babies in stories and in ads. Or I flip through the TV channels and see a diaper commercial. It could be that it's just top of mind, but it's weird how that happens.

I thought about adopting, but I wanted the birth experience. I wanted to feel my stomach tickle when the baby moved for the first time. I wanted to hear her scream when she was born. I wanted it all.

When Mike and I were together, we talked about having kids and what we would name them. He loved the name Jack. I loved the name Daisy. It was my great-grandmother's name, and I always wanted to have a girl and name her Daisy.

When I got back from lunch the next day, there was a vase of daisies on my desk. I knew exactly who had sent them. I opened the card.

You're going to be a wonderful mother. Thinking of you, Sue and Chloe

I called Sue to thank her for the flowers.

"So I think I settled on the semen."

Sue laughed. "Do you know how funny that sounds?"

"OK then, the donor. He's tall and thin, strawberry blonde hair, like me, and smart. No. 424."

"He's got a number?"

"Yeah. No name. Just a number."

"And the sperm's been tested and all that?" Sue asked.

"Yes. I mean he's been tested for all kinds of crap. But I'm sure the sperm's good or they wouldn't use it. Those little suckers have to be good swimmers."

"But not as good as if you were having regular sex, right?" Sue asked.

"True. They don't have as far to swim. The doctor will give them a good lead. But still, I don't think they use sub-par sperm. They want performers who have proven results."

"Omigod! I just thought of something. They won't get it mixed up, will they? Like give you a short, fat, bald man's?"

I laughed. "No."

"Good."

"Leave it up to you to worry about my sperm."

"Hey, I'm just looking out for you. Besides, you deserve good sperm. You've waited a long time."

I smiled.

"So when's the big sperm day anyway?"

"I'll probably start trying in a couple of months. After the reunion."

"So you're coming. You're really coming this time?"

Sue sounded as excited as a child who finds an extra prize in a box of Cracker Jacks.

"Yeah, I'll come home and go. But you have to go with me."

"Absolutely," Sue said. "It'll be like old times. Can't wait."

"What are you planning to wear?" I asked.

"The invitation says casual, so I'll probably wear slacks. It also said to bring mementos for the display table. I found my cheerleading jacket. It smells like mothballs. Mom had it in an old chest in the attic. And I also have the program from our senior class play and our homecoming court picture. If you have any stuff like that, bring it."

"The only thing I have is my yearbook."

"You don't have any photos of you and Mike or the squad?"

"Not anymore. But I'll ask Mom. Maybe she kept some."

When I got off the phone with Sue, I dug back into the criminal case I was working on. It dealt with a co-ed who claimed she had been raped repeatedly in various positions by two guys she met at a party. They, of course, claimed it was consensual.

The more I studied the case, the angrier I got. The guys took her to their dorm room and one blocked the door while the other one raped her. Then they swapped. I was going to go after these bastards. Someone had to stand up for those who couldn't, and I had decided a long time ago that it was going to be me.

Every time I prosecuted a case with a young girl, it brought back memories of that night. I had worked through all my demons, but sometimes, in the quiet of the night, they'd return just to show me they could. They'd taunt me and remind me that they had won.

I didn't speak up like the young girl in this case. I wasn't smart like she was; I didn't go to the hospital and get a rape exam. I allowed my voice to be silenced by a threat I was too young and naïve to believe.

For a long time, I wanted to confront Smith. I daydreamed about it. Usually I imagined that I'd show up in a public place where he was and confront him. I'd embarrass him in front of everyone. Then I'd watch him get smaller and smaller and smaller until he was no bigger than an ant and unable to hurt anyone. The ant-size Smith would scramble along the sidewalk trying to escape being smashed by my high heels. He'd make it into the grass and think he was safe among the sharp blades. But he wasn't.

I love running in bare feet through the grass.

****

Mike

I picked up Jack to take him to school on my way to work.

Jack crawled into the front seat and stashed his backpack between his legs.

"You look sleepy," I said.

He yawned. "You try sleeping with a baby in the next room. Paige is a pain. I don't know why Mom wanted another kid anyhow."

I smiled. "Ah come on, Jack. You were a baby once."

"Yeah, and Mom says I didn't cry like Paige does."

"You were a pretty good baby as I recall," I said. "Except the time you peed in my mouth."

Jack scrunched his freckled nose. "Eww! That's seriously gross, Dad."

"Tell me about it. I was changing your diaper, and as soon as I took off the soiled one, you let loose all over me. My mouth was open. Yeah, it was pretty gross."

Jack laughed. "What it taste like?"

I laughed. "That I don't remember, but it definitely didn't taste like anything I wanted to taste ever again. After that, I didn't take any chances. I threw a towel over you until I got the new diaper on."

"Did you ever want another kid?" Jack asked.

I pulled into the school. "Never really thought about it. I have you and you're enough to handle."

Jack opened the door and jumped out. He threw his black and red backpack over his left shoulder. "Bye, Dad."

I watched as he walked toward the entrance and disappeared through the glass doors. My boy was growing up so fast. Too fast.

I blinked back tears. Jack was so much like me that it scared me sometimes. Not that I was a bad kid, but I always had to learn everything the hard way. Just like Jack. I remember when he was around four, I told him not to touch the fireplace door because it was hot. Next thing I knew, he had touched the door. I thought Lisa was going to kill me when I dropped him off with both hands wrapped in bandages. But that's how Jack is. He always has to learn everything on his own. And I know how dangerous that can be.

As I pulled away from the curb, I glanced back at the school entrance. Truth was I had lied to Jack. I would have loved to have had more kids. I planned on it. But life had some different ideas.

****

"Large coffee, room for cream," I told the barista. I tilted the stainless steel carafe and poured half and half into my coffee. I heard a high-pitched voice and it sounded familiar. I turned around. It was Lynn Reynolds. I hadn't seen her since high school. First Cookie, now Lynn.

"Caramel latte," Lynn said.

"Is that you, Lynn?" I asked.

She turned around. "Oh. My. God. Mike Parker. How the hell are you?"

Yep. It was Lynn. Same squinty eyes and narrow nose.

She walked over and hugged me. "It's gotta be ten years."

She scanned me from my head to my feet, nodding in approval. "You look great."

"You, too," I said. "What are you doing here?"

Lynn sipped her latte. "I'm meeting with the country club staff to go over some reunion details. You are coming, aren't you?"

I grimaced. "Haven't decided. But now that I know you're planning it, maybe I will."

Lynn was our class president. She had planned our high school prom and made a career as an events planner in a town in the northeast part of the state where she went to college. Gina used to say how Lynn obsessed about the tiniest details. I remember Gina telling me how Lynn threw a party for her parents, who were birders. Everything had a bird theme. The party favors were natural twig bird nests filled with Godiva chocolate truffles. Gina always said that she wanted Lynn to help plan our wedding. God, I wish that had happened.

"You can come alone," Lynn said. "What I mean is, you can bring somebody, but if you don't have anybody you want to bring, still come. There are several people who are coming alone. So it's not like you have to be a couple to come. In fact, my husband, Jerry, will be in Germany on business so I'll be coming by myself."

"I'll think about it."

"I mean it, Mike. You'd better come. You haven't been to any of our reunions. This one's going to be the best yet. Promise!"

****

Gina

I couldn't wait to lace up my sneakers and head out the door when I got home from work. Pinching those two inches killed me. I went to Weight Watchers once and gave up after a few weeks of counting points. The points thing just wasn't for me. Besides, I figured I could lose fifteen pounds on my own if I really tried. I started running and watched the snacks and it worked. I figured a few weeks of running and watching what I ate would leave me a little slimmer by reunion time.

Running was also good thinking time. Whenever I ran, I let my mind wander. I often worked out problems or ran through cases as I exercised. I thought about my current case, the one involving the co-ed that I was preparing to present to a grand jury. The poor girl quit school to live at home and attend a community college. She was having a tough time but thankfully she reported the rape and got help immediately. I worked closely with the victim witness coordinator and detectives assigned to the case. Together, we'd bring these boys down.

The asphalt running path around the perimeter of the park wasn't very wide, maybe enough for two people to walk side by side. A guy was coming toward me with a chocolate lab and just as I went into the grass to pass them, I tripped and fell.

"Damn!"

The guy stopped. "Are you OK?"

He held out his free hand.

I waved it away. "Yeah. I'm such a klutz!" I got up and took a deep breath. I wiped my sweaty face with the small white cotton towel I always ran with.

"You don't seem like a klutz. I've watched you circle the park three times now. Each lap is about a mile and a half. So, I'd say you're working on mile five here."

I held out my hand. "Hi. I'm Gina. Gina McKenzie."

He nodded. "Rob Miller." He patted the dog. "And this is Molly."

The guy was steamy in his torn jeans and white button down shirt. He had short black hair peppered with gray around the temples. Thick brows and a dimple in the middle of his square chin. And straight teeth.

I reached down to pet Molly. "How old is she?"

"She's pushing 10. I got her when I was 30. She's the only lady who's ever stayed with me," he laughed.

"Do you come here every day?"

"Pretty much every day," he said. "We live close and can walk here. We moved in about six months ago."

"What kind of work do you do," I asked.

"Promise you won't laugh?"

"Promise."

"I'm a proctologist."

I couldn't help it. I laughed a little. "An ass doctor?"

He smiled. "You said you wouldn't laugh."

"I know. I know. Sorry. We do need ass doctors after all."

Rob laughed. "What about you? What do you do?"

"I'm a prosecutor."

"So what do you prosecute?" he asked.

"Sexual assault cases."

"That's intense."

"Yeah," I said. "But someone's got to put the bastards behind bars."

Rob nodded. "Well, we'd better get going. Maybe I'll see you here again. Sorry if I messed up your run."

"You didn't. It was nice meeting you, too."

As Rob and Molly walked away, I felt a tiny tingle that I hadn't felt since high school. It caught me off guard. I never thought I'd ever feel that tingle again, and certainly not after just meeting a guy for the first time. I went home thinking that I would have to run in the park more often.

****

I looked at the caller ID. "Hey, Mom. I was going to call you later. Did you get my email with the donor profiles?"

I heard Mom clear her throat. "Are you sure there's no other way, Gina?"

"Well, the only other way I know of is to find someone to screw. And finding a screwable guy that meets all of my requirements isn't easy."

"I know. I know," Mom said. "This just seems so, so unnatural."

"And picking someone off the street corner isn't? Look, Mom. I kissed a lot of frogs in my life and none of them were my prince. That's just the way it goes."

Mom wasn't about to let up. "What about a good friend?"

"Mom!" I shouted. "Are you suggesting I ask a good friend to get me pregnant?"

"Well. It might work. People do it in the movies."

"That comes with other complications. Like what if the good friend decides he wants to be a part of my baby's life?"

"Well, you're an attorney. Couldn't you get him to sign something?" Mom asked.

"Mom! And besides, all of my good male friends have wives or girlfriends and I don't think anyone would be willing to lend her man to me for a night or two."

"What about that gay friend of yours? He seems nice."

"Scott? He is nice. But I could never ask Scott, or any other gay man, to get me pregnant."

"I was just thinking that he might be willing. It's not like he needs his semen."

"Mom!"

"OK. OK. I guess it does sound pretty dumb."

"Yeah, Mom. But I love you. Look, I wish this wasn't the way it had to happen either, but I have no choice if I want a child of my own. And besides, you of all people should understand what I'm going through."

I was an only child. Mom and Dad had adopted me as a baby after trying to have one of their own for years.

"You're right, Gina. Let's just hope it works. I'll pray for good semen. And I'll get all of my friends to pray for good semen."

Mom made me laugh. She had a funny way of phrasing things.

"I've decided to come home for the reunion," I told her. "You gonna be around that weekend?"

Mom checked her calendar. "Bad news. That's the Saturday I'm going on the overnight bus trip to New York. But I can cancel."

"Don't you dare cancel. I'll fly home Friday and spend the day with you before your New York trip. I won't be around Saturday anyhow if I go to the reunion."

"Are you sure?"

"Positive."

****

Mike

Jack was waiting for me on the curb in front of the school. I pulled up, and he opened the door and climbed in.

"How was your day, bud?"

Jack sighed. "OK."

"Just OK?"

Jack looked like a deflated balloon. His eyes scrunched and he grimaced like he had struck out, dashing his team's hopes for a come-from-behind win.

"Well, I kind of didn't do too well on my spelling test today," he said.

"What'd ya get?"

Jack shook his head. "I don't want to say."

"It can't be that bad."

Jack nodded. "Trust me, it is."

"70?"

"Lower."

"65?"

"Lower."

"Lower than a 65? Geez, Jack. Didn't you study?"

"I kind of got an F?"

"F?" My voice jumped a few octaves. "OK, Jack, what happened?"

"I forgot to study, and I figured that I could cheat, just this one time. Turned out Miss Sharp caught me and I got an automatic F."

Inside I was smiling because I had done the same thing when I was Jack's age and got caught, too. But the father in me knew I had to handle this moment in a fatherly way. "Well, guess that'll teach you not to cheat."

Jack's eyebrows arched. "So you're not mad?"

"Of course I'm mad. Disappointed is probably a better word. Have fun telling your mom when you get home."

"Do I have to tell her?"

"What'd you think?"

Jack was quick on the draw. "No. I don't think she needs to know."

I smiled. "Think again Jack-ster."

"Dang! Mom will go parental on me. She hates cheaters. Every time I try to cheat in Monopoly, she catches me."

"But wouldn't you rather be the one to tell her and not your teacher?"

Jack sighed. "I suppose. I wish I could start today over."

I rubbed the top of Jack's head. "Some days are like that, bud. It's called life."

Jack shifted in his seat. "Oh, forgot to tell you. Mom said that you should go to your high school reunion."

"Oh, yeah? How does she know about that?"

"She ran into someone who went to school with you and they mentioned it. Mom said she hopes that you go; something about Gina."

"She mentioned Gina?"

"Yeah. Who's Gina?"

"Just someone I went to school with?"

"Was she your girlfriend?"

"Yeah."

"Was she hot?"

"Jack!"

"Just asking if she was hot, dad. Geez."

"Yes, she was pretty." I looked at Jack. "OK, Hot. She was pretty hot."

I dropped Jack off at Lisa's and went home. I picked up the reunion invitation and read it again. Oh, what the hell. Guess I'll go. Even if I don't stay for very long, as least I can say I went. And it might be nice to see some of the old gang again. Most of them moved away after high school.

Chapter 9

Gina

Every day, I'd run after work and I'd look for Rob. I felt like a pathetic teenager with raging hormones, but I wanted to see if I felt that tingle again or if it was just a freak thing. I call the tingle The Mike Effect.

I've been with a few guys since Mike, and none of them made me feel the tingle. We had OK sex, but nothing that wowed me like when I was with Mike. Even the first time Mike and I did it, it wasn't as bad as most of my friends had told me it would be. We were both virgins, and Mike was so gentle.

I remember the night so well. You never forget the night you lose your virginity. We were under our make-out tree on his sleeping bag. We were all over each other, and I felt like I was going to die I wanted him so badly. My body quivered and I felt

100

his hardness against me. I couldn't take it anymore. I pulled him toward me.

"Gina, baby, are you sure?" Mike asked, stopping to hold my face still so he could look me in the eyes and see that I really meant what I was guiding him to do.

"Yes, please. I want to."

"God, baby, I love you." And Mike was kissing me in places I never knew could bring me so much pleasure.

He grabbed the condom he had brought, just in case, and I heard it rip open.

"I don't want to hurt you, baby. If I am, please tell me and I'll stop."

Mike eased his way into me all the while kissing me and telling me how much he loved me and wanted me. I felt a little pang but it didn't hurt as much as I thought it would. Mike came so hard I thought he was hurt. And it was the first and only time I didn't have an orgasm. After that, things got pretty incredible pretty fast and sex with Mike was like a drug I could never get enough of.

****

I was about ready to give up on Rob when he and Molly turned the corner. I saw Molly's head before I saw Rob.

My pink shirt was soaked with sweat and I was sure I reeked, but I stopped to whisper a breathless hello.

"Whoa, Molly!" Rob pulled slightly on Molly's leash so she would stop. "I was hoping to see you here."

I wiped the sweat off my forehead with my running towel. "Really?"

"Yeah, I … I wondered if you'd like to get coffee sometime."

I huffed. "Coffee?"

"Yeah."

"I'm more of a tea girl."

Rob laughed. "OK. Tea for you and coffee for me."

I huffed. "When?"

"Is tonight too soon?" he asked. "I'm headed out of town tomorrow."

"Sure. Tonight's great. When and where?"

"Nine at the diner on the corner of Park and Roosevelt?"

I nodded. "See you then."

I picked up speed and ran as fast as I could the rest of the way home. I couldn't believe that I had just accepted an invitation for coffee from someone I barely knew. But it was in a public place so that made me feel better. One of the things I've had to work on with my therapist is trust issues. Ever since the rape, it's hard for me to trust any guy. If I were honest, that's why the few relationships I've had didn't last.

I was dripping like an ice-cream cone in the sun and just as sticky. I tore off my drenched clothes and jumped into the tiled shower. I liked Rob, even if he was an ass doctor. And coffee was innocent enough. It wasn't a whole dinner so I wouldn't be stuck for long if he turned out to be a frog. And he wasn't picking me up; I was meeting him there, which was good. I didn't like guys picking me up at my place on the first date; I had to make sure they were all right before I gave them my address. And I always ran criminal checks on them, which I had already done the day after I met Rob. The only things I found were a couple of parking tickets.

"You clean up nice," Rob said as I approached the corner booth with the candy apple red vinyl seats and white piping. The diner looked like it hadn't changed much since the 1950s. The tables were original with metal banding and chrome column bases. I laughed to myself because people pay a mint to duplicate the retro look in their homes and here was the real-deal.

"Thanks. I hope I smell better."

Rob inhaled. "You smell good. Much better than you did earlier. I mean, uh. Not that you smelled that bad before, but you smell better now." He pulled on his earlobe. "God, I'm an idiot."

I laughed. It was fun to watch a guy squirm in social awkwardness.

The waitress came over. She was a young girl with pigtails, saddle shoes and bobby socks and a pink and black poodle skirt. Guess it went with the diner's retro look. I noticed a hula-hoop hanging on the wall along with a pair of white roller skates and a high school letter jacket. A jukebox sat in the corner. The owner was smart to capitalize on nostalgia. People love reliving their youth, and from the age and crowd in the diner, I'd say it was working.

"Can I get you something?" the young girl asked.

"Tea, please. Earl Grey if you have it."

The girl bounced away.

Rob sipped his coffee while his eyes lingered on mine. "So what else besides tea do you like?"

"I love cheese pizza and reading and running and traveling and winning."

"Winning?"

"Yeah, I like to win my cases."

"Ever lose?" Rob asked.

"A couple of times."

"How'd it feel?"

"Lousy. The bastards deserved to be behind bars. Enough about me. What about you. Did you ever lose a patient?"

Rob looked down table. "Yeah, a few."

He gripped his coffee mug tighter and his body stiffened.

"What made you go into medicine?" I asked, wanting to get off the whole death thing because it obviously bothered him.

"Guess I always wanted to help people. I had a friend who had Crohn's disease and that's what got me interested in the specialty."

"Was it hard?" I asked, dipping my tea bag into my mug.

"Very hard. There were times when I didn't think I would make it. I used to have this nightmare where I would wake up and be late for an important exam."

"Were you?"

"What?"

"Ever late."

"No," Rob said. "But I always set two alarm clocks 10 minutes apart just in case the one would fail or I'd fall back to sleep."

"So at least you were prepared."

"Yeah, you could say that. But maybe a little obsessed."

Rob took another sip and smiled. He had straight teeth, and it made me chuckle because it reminded me of what was noted on the sperm donor's profile.

"So, want to go out on a real date sometime?" he asked.

"That would be nice."

"Are you free this weekend?"

"Actually, I'm flying home for my 20th high school reunion. I can't believe it's been that long."

Rob nodded. "I know what you mean. I had my 25th last year. It was the first one I was able to make."

"This will be my first, too."

"Where are you from?"

"Pennsylvania."

"That's a long way from Florida. I'm from the northeast, too. Vermont. How'd you end up in Florida anyway?"

"It's a long story. The short version is that I was offered a job out of law school in the sex crimes division in Miami. All of the other offers were from places in the northeast. I'm not crazy about snow and ice, so I picked Miami. I was ready for a change of scenery. Got here and never left. What about you?"

"Honestly, I never thought I would be living in Florida. It's a world apart from Vermont. But one thing led to another and I ended up where I had the best offer. I try to make it back to Vermont in the winter to spend time with my parents and ski some of my old stomping grounds. So when are you coming back from Pennsylvania?"

I poured some hot water into my mug and opened a fresh tea bag. "I'll be back the following weekend."

Rob checked the calendar on his phone. "I'm free on that Saturday. Does that work for you?"

I nodded.

"I'll pick you up this time. Say around 7?" he smiled.

We talked through three cups of tea and then Rob walked me home. It turned out that I was as many blocks to the west of the diner and he was to the east. I looked up at the spring sky. Clouds veiled the stars. A twinkling light from a plane caught my eye as it crossed the sky. "I always wonder where people are flying to."

Rob looked up. "When I was a kid, whenever I'd see a plane in the sky, I'd imagine that I was on the plane and it was taking me on a secret adventure."

"What kind of adventure?"

"The little boy kind, with bears and tigers and cowboys and Indians."

"Sounds dangerous."

"It was," Rob said. "But I always made it home safely."

He looked at me and shook his head. "I can't believe I'm telling you all this, Gina. I didn't mean to bore you. You're so easy to talk to."

I smiled. "You're not boring me. I'm enjoying it."

We arrived at my apartment building, a luxury high-rise located minutes from downtown Miami and the Metrorail. I loved my unit on the seventh floor because it had an oversized balcony.

Rob looked at me and I thought for a second he was going to lean in and kiss me. Instead, he held out his hand. "Thanks, Gina."

"Thank you," I responded. "For both the tea and the conversation. It was great getting to know you better."

Rob smiled. "See you in two weekends, right?"

I nodded. "Thanks for walking me home."

"No problem. I'll call you next week after you get back. If you need to reach me before then, here's my number."

He handed me his business card. "My personal cell's on the back."

I took the card and slid it inside my purse. "It's been a long time since I've been on a date."

"Me, too," he said. "So I guess this will be a treat for both of us."

I smiled. "Thanks again for the talk and tea."

He waited until I got inside the door before turning to walk away. I scrambled up the stairs to my apartment and watched him walk away. I liked him. He was easy going, kind of like a comfortable pair of shoes that fit just right without having to break them in. I was definitely looking forward to getting to know Rob better.

****

Mike

When Jack called to say goodnight, I asked how his mom took the news about him getting the F.

"She said no video games for a few days. She thinks I'm playing too many games and not doing my school work."

"Are you?"

"I play games but I do study. But maybe not as much as I should."

"Well, guess your mom has a point then."

"Maybe a little one."

When I got off the phone with Jack, I remembered the time in high school that Gina and

I went skiing the night before a huge chemistry test. The school ski club had planned the outing for weeks, and I was so pissed that the teacher scheduled the exam for that day. My buddies and I tried to get her to reschedule, but Mrs. You're-in-school-to-learn-not-to-play wouldn't. So, I went skiing and bombed the test. Mom and Dad went ape shit on me. Gina, on the other hand, got an A. She always got A's. Even in math and she totally sucked in math.

I wondered if I would see Gina at the reunion, and if I did, what I would say to her. Maybe she wouldn't talk to me. Or maybe I'd have to be the one to start the conversation. Just thinking about her made my groin ache like it did when I was a scrawny teen and only had to shave once a week. She's the only girl I've ever dated that made me feel this way.

Lisa was great. She was, or is, beautiful and smart. But Lisa was right when she told me at the end of our marriage that she couldn't compete with Gina any longer, even if it was just a memory.

Jack was maybe one at the time and we had just gotten home from visiting Lisa's parents in Connecticut.

"I'm sorry, Mike," Lisa cried that night. "I thought I could make you love me the way you loved her. But that's never going to happen. I know that now."

"Christ, Lisa. I'm so sorry. I never meant to hurt you."

"I know," she said. "I should never have forced the marriage. Deep down I knew you still loved her but I thought if I loved you enough that it wouldn't matter. But it does. I want more. I know that now."

"And you deserve more," I told her. "You deserve someone who will love you the way you deserve to be loved. I'm sorry I wasn't that guy. But God, Lisa, please know that Jack means everything to me. You gave me him, and I will never forget that."

I hated myself for what I did to Lisa. She deserved better, and I felt guilty that I couldn't give her what she needed. I thought I could. We had a great time for a while. But in the end, no matter how hard I tried, it wasn't enough for her. I knew it even before she said it. Letting Lisa go, as hard as it was, felt right. I was happy when she married the dentist she worked for as a hygienist. It was obvious in the way he treated her and the things he bought her that he adored her. Worshipped is probably a better word. And he was good to Jack.

****

Gina

I parked the black Audi I had rented in the back row of the parking lot at the hotel. I had a clear view of the ballroom entrance. I didn't recognize many of my classmates as they walked toward the ornate double doors. Every time I reached to open the car door, I stopped. My heart pounded and my throat tightened. I needed a stiff drink. Something to take the edge off. I just wasn't sure I could walk into the ballroom alone.

There was a knock on the driver's side window and I shrieked and jumped in my seat, hitting my head on the car ceiling.

It was Tom. I'd recognize that dimpled smile anywhere. I rolled down the window.

Tom bent over, his George Clooney head inches from mine. "Hi, Gina. Mind if I join you?"

I unlocked the passenger door and Tom walked around to the other side and slid in.

"My god, it has to be..."

"Twenty years," he smiled. "I see your mom, though, when she picks up her cholesterol medicine."

"Yeah, she says she sees you at the drug store and walking your dog in the park."

Tom smiled. "Klondike, my dog, loves the park." He patted his stomach. "And it's good for me, too. Did you come alone?"

"Sue was supposed to come with me but she had to do something with her daughter, Chloe, first. She'll be here later. I'm supposed to go in awhile."

Tom cocked his head. "So what's stopping you?"

His blue gray eyes met mine. "I don't know. I thought I could do this. I really did. But now I'm not so sure."

"What are you afraid of, Gina?" Tom asked.

"Afraid of? Not really afraid of anything. Just feel awkward. I mean, I haven't been back since I left, except to visit Mom. I'm not sure I belong here anymore. Or if the others will even like me."

"Gina, you can always come home," Tom said. "Just because you moved away to pursue your career and do your own thing doesn't mean you're not one of us. You'll always be one of us."

I patted Tom's hand. "Thanks, Tom. You always did have a way of making me feel better." I laughed. "Remember those unknowns in chemistry?"

Tom smiled and nodded. "Sure do. I saved your ass more than once in that class."

"You're so right. I was pathetic when it came to figuring those substances out."

Tom narrowed his eyes and sighed. He opened his mouth like he was going to talk, only he didn't say anything.

"What is it, Tom? You look like you want to say something."

"I do but I don't want to upset you."

"Upset me. Why would anything you say upset me?"

"Well, I have a question I've wanted to ask you for a long time. Something that's bothered me for twenty years."

"Ask away."

"Maybe we could get together before you leave?" he said. "I'm not sure this is the time or the place to have this discussion."

I looked at Tom. He pushed up on his wire-rim glasses.

"Oh, no. You're not going to get away with that. Now you have me curious. What question could be that important that you had it for twenty years?"

"I'm not sure tonight's the night, Gina."

I slapped my lap. "Yes, tonight is the night. Now I'm way too curious to wait another second. What is it?"

"It's about that night."

"What night?"

"The night that Coach Smith did what he did to you."

My mouth fell open. I couldn't speak. My heart raced and I could feel my skin warming up. Tears pooled in my eyes

"Don't worry," said Tom, taking off his glasses to dab his glassy eyes with the palm of his hand. "I never told anyone. But I wanted to. That bastard deserved to be punished. But I told myself that it was up to you to tell, not me. And if you didn't want to tell anyone, then I had to respect that. Besides, I didn't want to make things harder for you."

I shook my head. "But how…"

"How did I know?"

I nodded.

"That night. The night you were babysitting for Coach Smith and his wife, I was out for a run through the neighborhood. I lived several streets over from them. I turned the corner to see you get into your car and speed away. Then I saw Coach Smith stumble down his driveway waving a pair of pink bikini underwear and mumbling. I stopped running and dragged him into his house. When I realized what he had done to you, I punched him in the face. A couple of times."

I remember seeing Coach Smith at the gas station days later and his eye was black and blue. "So that's where the black eye came from?" I asked.

Tom nodded. "He bragged about what he did to you and I told him that if he ever laid a hand on you ever again, I would kill him. And I meant it. When he told me that you wouldn't say anything because of his threat to do something to Mike, I knew you wouldn't. I knew you loved Mike too much. It was so hard for me not to say anything, Gina. I wanted to tell Mike. Maybe I should have. But I just kept thinking that it was your secret to tell, not mine. And I was mad for a long time that you hadn't told anyone. Even after the baseball season was over and the bastard couldn't hurt Mike anymore you kept quiet."

"And you never told anyone?" I asked him again.

"No. Like I said, I wanted to lots of times. Whenever I'd run into Coach Smith, I'd stare him down just so the bastard knew that I hadn't forgotten."

I couldn't believe my ears. "So why bring this up now?"

"I don't know," Tom said. "Because you're here and we're alone and we can talk. And it's bothered me for a long time, and I've always cared about you and want to make sure you're all right."

"I'm OK. But it hasn't been easy. A big reason I became a prosecutor in the sex crimes unit was to put people like him away. I kind of feel like each time I'm in court and the outcome is in my favor I not only win for the victim but also for me. You're right. I should have said something. I was a naïve 17-year-old who thought that Smith really had the power to ruin Mike's life. It wasn't until I was older that I realized that I was the one who had the power, that if I had reported what he had done, Smith would have been done for and Mike would have had another coach. I was so stupid."

"No, you weren't stupid," Tom said. "You were seventeen. And besides, if you were stupid, I was stupid, too. I should have talked to you about it then, but I just couldn't. But I've waited twenty years to tell you I'm sorry. Sorry that I wasn't a better friend."

My eyes were swimming in tears. I couldn't help leaning over and hugging Tom. "You've always been a great friend. Just look at all of those unknowns you solved for me?"

Tom smiled. "Yeah, guess that's true."

"Besides," I hit his arm playfully, "you're not the only friend who's upset with the way I handled the situation."

"But I thought you never told anyone," Tom said.

"I didn't, until last night when I confided in Sue. She went ballistic. Cussed a firestorm of words I never heard coming out of her mouth before. She said if she would have known what he had done she would have made me tell."

"Good for her," Tom said.

"Enough about me. What about you. Why haven't you ever married?"

"Never found the right girl. There was this girl in high school that I always liked. You know her well. She was always dating someone else, though, and I never had a chance."

"And who would that be?" I asked.

Tom put his glasses back on. "Sue."

"So why not ask her out?"

"I don't know. For one thing, every time I see her she's always in a hurry."

"That's just Sue. She's a ball of energy. Remember we called her Tigger in school because she was always bouncing?"

Tom smiled. "I had forgotten about that. But I also rarely see her."

"That's no excuse," I said. "Pick up the phone. You're a big boy."

"I know. But for some reason around her I can't seem to get the words out. Christ, I'm almost forty and I still get that way."

I smiled. I had no idea Tom had carried the torch for Sue for so long, and I knew that Sue had no idea.

"Tell ya what. She's coming later. Hang with me and maybe you'll get comfortable enough to ask her."

I felt like I was back in high school playing matchmaker. And I wouldn't have offered if I didn't think Sue would be interested, but I knew that she would be. Just the other night we had talked about high school and the guys we would have dated and Tom was on her list. Sue said she always thought he was nice. Now it was just a matter of getting them both together. And I knew I could do that.

****

Mike

I pulled into the hotel parking lot and parked beside Jeremy's red Mustang. He was probably on his second gin and tonic. I didn't drink much anymore and, when I did, it was a Yuengling lager. I turned off the car and looked into the rear-view mirror. Nothing hanging out of my nose; good. I grinned. Nothing sticking to my teeth; good. I remember one date I had a piece of green lettuce sticking to my front tooth and didn't realize it until I got home and went to brush my teeth. My date never said anything; it might just be why she turned me down when I called to set up a second date.

I reached for the door handle and looked in the side view mirror. Sue pulled in behind me. I opened the door just as she was turning off her car. She tooted the horn.

I turned around and waved and Sue held up her index finger and mouthed "Wait!"

She grabbed her purse and hopped out of the car. "Michael Parker. I wondered if I'd see you here."

She hugged me like we were old buds and I instinctively put my arms around her.

I nodded toward the door. "I was just about ready to go in. Want to go in together?"

Sue smiled. "Sure. I'm supposed to meet Gina here, but she's probably already inside."

Sue scanned the parking lot. "I don't see her Audi."

Just hearing Gina's name made my heart skip a beat. I had wondered if she was coming and now that I knew that she was, I was scared as hell to see her. I had practiced bumping into her in front of the mirror all week, practicing what I would say, how I would smile. And now I'd see if all of my practice paid off. I took a deep breath and walked with Sue to the front door. The closer we got to the door, the sweatier my palms got.

"Save me a dance, OK?" Sue said. "You always were the best dancer. You and Gi..."

She stopped in mid-sentence.

"Sorry. I didn't mean…"

"It's OK. It's been 20 years. You're right. Gina and I were pretty good dancers."

Sue slipped in the door and I followed her, stopping at the table right inside to sign in and get our nametags.

"Sue and Mike," Lynn said, coming out from behind the table to hug us both. "I'm so glad you came."

She waved her arm toward the other end of the room. "There's an open bar and some munchies to hold you over until dinner."

Lynn looked at Sue. "Gina told me to tell you that she's over at the mementoes table with Tom. You're to head over there."

Sue started to walk away and then stopped and turned around. "Are you coming?"

"With you?" I asked.

"Yes, with me." Sue held out her hand. "Don't you want to see Tom and Gina?"

I nodded. "Sure." If my hands were sweaty before, they were drenched now. I stuck them inside my pockets to wipe them off.

Sue hadn't changed. She was always a take-charge-kind-of-girl.

"Sue! Sue! Over here."

We glanced in the direction of the voice. "It's Karen," Sue said.

Karen rushed over and hugged Sue and looked at me and squinted. "Michael Parker?"

I nodded.

"Omigod. You haven't changed one bit. Well, except for the gray around the temples but it makes you look sexier."

A girl was with Karen and she looked like a runway model – tall and thin and dark eyes that looked Asian.

"Mia, this is Sue and Mike."

Mia held out her hand to shake ours. She had long fingers and her nails were painted a deep red. She wore a band of diamonds on her left ring finger, so I figured she must be married.

"Mia is my partner," Karen explained.

Holy shit, I thought to myself. I had no idea Karen was gay and this chick, her partner, was drop dead gorgeous. I coughed and tried to recover with a smile.

Sue smiled. "Gina told me you two had a son."

Karen smiled and dug a small blue photo album out of her purse. She opened it. "This is Will."

Sue took the album to get a closer look. "He's so cute! Looks like you, Mia."

Mia smiled. "Thanks. We used my egg."

"And I carried him," said Karen, smiling at Mia.

Sue held the album up so I could see the photo of Will.

I nodded. Will did look like Mia. Same shiny black hair and almond-shaped eyes. I was trying to take in the whole sight. This is the same girl who got pregnant our senior year, had her baby that summer and married the dad. I had heard they split not long after they married, but I had no idea that she preferred girls. Damn, the shit you miss.

Someone I didn't recognize came up to talk to Karen and Mia and Sue and I headed toward Gina and Tom. The closer we got the faster my heart beat. I wiped my sweaty palms again. Damn, just thinking about her made me crazy – still!

Chapter 10

Mike

Gina stood in front of a display table leaning forward to look at photos on a board. Even from a distance I recognized her figure. Her long legs and arms, and tiny waist. She looked beautiful in a brown silk dress and high heels. Her red hair fell down her back in waves.

Tom saw us first. He touched Gina's arm and whispered in her ear and Gina turned and looked toward us. Her eyes met mine and hung on.

Sue put her arm around me. "Lookie who I found in the parking lot?"

Tom held out his hand. "Great to see you, Mike. And you, too, Sue."

Gina hugged Sue and then turned to me. I wanted to hug Gina but I thought maybe that was too much, so I held out my hand to shake hers instead.

Gina smiled her gorgeous, smile. "Hi, Mike. You're looking good."

"You, too."

Gina nodded toward the display table. "We were just looking at photos from high school."

"Any of me up there?" Sue asked.

Gina nodded. "There's one of you cheering."

"Oh God, let me see." Sue squeezed in next to Gina to look at the photos.

"How's the pharmacy thing going?" I asked Tom.

"Busy. The older people keep us in business."

"Yeah, guess people are living longer, which means more prescriptions, which means more business."

"That's about right. How about you? How's the electricity business?"

"OK. It's something that people always need so that's good. Keeps me in a job."

Sue turned around. "Here's one of you, Mike. You look like a doofus."

I walked over to look at the photos. I had to stand beside Gina because there wasn't enough room to squeeze in on the other side of Sue. Someone squeezed in on the other side of me, forcing me even closer to Gina. We were inches apart.

I could smell Gina's perfume. After twenty years, that musky scent still drove me wild. The smell was so powerful that it immediately transported me to our make-out place in the woods. We were on the sleeping bag and Gina's head was on my bare chest, her red hair fanned out, tickling my mid-section.

Christ, I wanted to grab her right there in the ballroom and kiss her. Maybe even ditch the reunion and find a place where we could be alone. I wondered what she felt, if she felt anything at all.

****

Gina

When I turned around and saw Mike, my heart danced. The tingle was back. Damn that tingle. Even after twenty years, he still made me feel like the only place to be was in his arms – and in his bed. His sexy smile made me dizzy with desire. The Mike Effect.

His teeth were just as white as I remembered them. He always had great teeth, and I remember I used to get mad because, unlike me, he never got cavities.

I watched as he shook Tom's hand. I wondered if he would shake my hand. What I really wanted him to do was to take me in his arms and kiss me. But he held out his hand and shook mine instead. Why did I ever let him go? I was so stupid, so young. God, I was getting wet just thinking about him, about us. No one has ever had this effect on me.

Except for a little graying around his temples, he hadn't changed much. I smiled when I saw the chicken pox scar on his cheek. Weird how a scar can mark you forever. It might smooth out over time, but the indentation remains. It never quite disappears.

He got that scar in kindergarten when he picked at a chicken pox. I used to trace the scar, about the size of a pencil eraser, with my finger and then trail down to his lips and circle them. Then he'd stick out his tongue and tickle my finger and I'd slip it inside his mouth and he would suck on it.

God, the damn stuff you remember. It all comes back so fast, and even if you think you're prepared for it, you never really are. Those damn waves, nailing you from behind, knocking you down, rolling you over and over until you're on the beach gasping for air.

"Hey, Mike," Sue said. "Remember in first grade you and I sang the opening to 'Rudolph the Red-nosed Reindeer?'

"I remember."

I wasn't in their first-grade class, but I had heard the story often.

"Everyone stood behind us on stage and they cupped their hands over their noses. Mike and I sang the introduction. You know Dasher and Dancer and Prancer and Vixen, Comet and Cupid and Donner and Blitzen. But do you recall the most famous reindeer of all? And then everyone uncovered their noses to show that they each had a red nose and joined in the singing, 'Rudolph the Red-nosed Reindeer.'"

Everyone laughed. I noticed how Tom's eyes clung to Sue. It was as if he were afraid to lose sight of her for fear she'd bounce away – again. He was so smitten.

"Anyway," said Sue, holding up a class photo. "Here's a photo of our first-grade class. I found it in the box of photos my mom kept."

Mike took the photo and smiled. "I was so dorky looking."

"We all were," Sue said.

Mike handed the photo back. "Can I get you girls something to drink?"

"A glass of chardonnay for me," Sue said.

"What about you, Gina?" Tom asked.

"How about a gin and tonic? But with diet tonic."

Tom nodded and left with Mike to get the drinks.

Sue grabbed my arm and flashed her big bug eyes at me. "Oh. My. God. Seeing you and Mike side by side was a blast from the past. You two look the same, only a little older."

"Thanks."

"Well, you know what I mean. You look good together. Think maybe…"

"I don't know. I still feel things for him, but I'm not sure he does for me. And there is so much to explain, I'm not sure where to begin."

"Start by telling him the truth."

I knew that Sue was referring to the rape. I've never seen her spit bullets like she had last night when I finally told her the truth.

"Can we talk about something else? Like the fact that I know something that you don't know," I said in a sing-songy voice.

"What? What? Tell me." Sue said, jumping up and down like a kid at an ice-cream truck.

"Tom likes you."

Sue's jaw dropped. "Tom, as in the Tom who was just here and went to get us drinks Tom?"

"Yep, that one. So what do you think?"

"Think? I think he's incredibly sexy but I had no idea he was interested in me."

"I know. That's why I'm telling you now. So you can warm up to him. He's a little on the shy side. He confessed his feelings earlier when we chatted in my car. He told me that he's liked you since high school but that he never got the chance to ask you out because you always had a boyfriend. I told him now's his chance."

"Omigod. Do I look all right? There's nothing hanging out of my nose or sticking on my teeth, is there?"

Sue smiled so I could see her teeth and leaned toward me so I could check her nose. "You look great. There's nothing hanging out of your nose and nothing sticking to your teeth."

"What about this pimple?" Sue pointed to a small bump on her chin. "Is the cover-up still on?

Of all the freakin' days to wake up with a zit on my chin!"

"The pimple looks great."

"Sure?" Sue asked. "It seemed to grow a lot today. I wanted to pop it."

"The pimple is perfect," I told her. "Besides, everyone has a few flaws. It's what makes us human."

Sue lowered her head to her armpits and sniffed. "Good. Deodorant's still working."

****

Mike

"So what do you think of the girls?" Tom asked.

"They're as gorgeous as ever. You and Gina aren't a…"

Tom made a stop sign with his hand. "Oh, no. We just walked in together. We pulled into the parking lot at the same time. Thinking about asking her out?"

"Not sure she'd go out," I told him.

"That's what I think about Sue."

"You're interested in Sue?"

"I've always been interested in Sue. It's just that she's always had a boyfriend. And when she got divorced and I'd see her, I was always too shy to ask her out. She always seems to be hurrying somewhere."

"That's Sue."

"Funny, that's what Gina said."

"So Gina knows you like Sue?"

"Kind of spilled my guts to her earlier. Just sort of came out."

"Well, my guess is that by now Sue knows."

"That quick?"

I nodded. "They're not soul sisters for nothing."

We were at the front of the line. "Two gin and tonics. Make one diet."

The bartended scanned the bottles. "Sorry, no diet."

Tom nudged me. "Just get the regular. Gina won't know the difference."

"Are you kidding me?" I said. "Gina will know the difference. She's not someone you can fool. I would never want to be on the other side of the courtroom."

"One gin and tonic and one Miller Lite draft," I told the bartender. I turned to Tom. "If she doesn't want the drink, I'm guessing she'll go for the beer."

Tom smirked. "And how confident are you about that?"

"I have zero confidence," I said. "With Gina, just when you think you have something figured out, she throws you a curve ball. I've never been sure why. I always thought that it's because she could, not because she really wanted to."

By the time we got back to Gina and Sue with the drinks, they were decades deep in conversation with Jeremy and his wife, Teresa.

Jeremy nodded at me. "I wondered when you'd get here. I was afraid you'd change your mind and not come."

"Well, I'm here," I said. I held up both drinks to Gina and explained about the diet.

Gina pursed her lips, her eyes drifting from one glass to the other. "Hmm. I think I'll get a wine."

The damn curve ball, I thought.

Lynn turned on the microphone and it made a high-pitched squeal that got everyone's attention.

"I grabbed a table near the dance floor," Jeremy said. "There's enough room for all of us."

We all followed Jeremy to the round table. Sue and Gina sat next to each other. I ended up on the other side of Gina and Tom ended up beside Sue. I winked at Tom. He and Sue looked good together.

"I want to welcome everyone to our 20th class reunion," Lynn said.

Woots and applause thundered in the cavernous ballroom, decorated in our school colors, orange and black.

"I can't believe that we've been out of school for 20 years," Lynn said. "It seems like only yesterday that Eric was luring Mrs. Hoffman into telling stories from her childhood."

People shouted "Yeah, Eric!" and clapped.

"And it seems like only yesterday Gina and Sue were leading the cheerleading squad," she continued.

Jeremy, Tom and I whipped our napkins in the air and cheered. Gina and Sue looked at one another and smiled.

"And we can't forget the time Jeremy, aka Bean, brought vodka to school in a soda bottle and passed out in the bathroom."

Teresa hit Jeremy. "You did what? If our kids ever did that you'd go berserk!"

"And good old Frank who drove the teachers crazy because he slept through most classes but somehow managed to get A's."

Lynn reminisced a few more minutes, telling some stories we'd probably rather forget, and then the meal began.

"That was nice that Maggie said the prayer and Cookie remembered all those who had died," Gina said. "I knew about Julie and Doug, but I didn't know about the other two."

One of our classmates had died of leukemia and the other from a brain aneurysm. He dropped over one morning. His wife found him on the bathroom floor, and he was kept on life support until they could harvest the organs.

Cookie explained that his wife got to meet the man who got her husband's heart and how much it meant to her to feel it beat again. I don't think there was a dry eye at our table after that story.

"I wondered why there were pamphlets on organ donation at the sign-in table," Sue said.

Sitting beside Gina was ten times tougher than I thought it would be. After all these years, she still turned me on. Damn, my groin ached. I couldn't believe that she still had this effect on me. I watched her slender fingers reach for her water glass. Her wrist was so tiny I could wrap my thumb and index finger around it and overlap them. She didn't wear a lot of makeup, which I liked. I hated when women wore so much makeup you couldn't see their skin. I preferred the natural look, like Gina. A touch of eye shadow and mascara emphasized her gorgeous green eyes.

I smiled when I saw Gina start to eat her salad. Some things never change. She always ordered her salad dressing on the side and dipped her fork into the dressing and then stabbed the lettuce. She said you didn't use as much salad dressing that way. Me, I'd pour the whole cup over the salad and then mixed it with my fork.

I leaned over to Gina. "Still take the dressing on the side, eh?"

Gina smiled. "There are some things that never change."

And she dipped her fork into the dressing and stabbed a cherry tomato. I watched as she bit the cherry tomato and sucked it before taking it in her mouth.

Christ. Watching her eat gave me a hard-on. God, I had it bad for this woman.

****

Gina

I was a little nervous when Mike pulled out the chair for me. I mean, it wasn't like we were a couple or anything. But I guess pulling out the chair doesn't mean we are a couple, I just wouldn't want anyone to think we were. I know I'm not making sense, but that's what he does to me. I get flustered.

I can stand in front of a jury and judge and be confident and cool and commanding. But when it comes to Mike, just being next to him makes me wobbly and weak in the knees. And horny as hell. No guy has ever made me feel the way he does. It's like my insides are being tickled.

"So, Gina," Jeremy said. "Sue tells us you're one hell of a prosecutor."

I looked at Sue. "I guess I'm not bad."

"Not bad," said Sue, her voice rising. "Gina's being modest. She's one of the best there is. And she's also going to make the best mommy."

I glared at Sue. She still blabs when she drinks.

Sue put her hand to her lips. "Oops! I wasn't supposed to say that."

"Do you have something to tell us?" Jeremy asked. "Does this call for a toast?"

"No," I said. "I think what Sue meant was that I would like a child. I'm exploring options."

"Like adoption?" Teresa asked.

"Perhaps."

"Artificial insemination?" Teresa asked.

"Teresa," Jeremy said. "I don't think Gina wants to talk about it."

"It's OK. Really. I've always wanted to be a mother so, you know, I might just do it a different way than you all have."

I didn't even want to look at Mike. My face felt hot so I knew it was probably fire-engine red. I wondered what he was thinking. He had a son. He got to be the dad he always wanted to be. In a way, I guess that made me mad. Stupid, I know. But that's how I felt.

Sue changed the topic before it went any further. "Hey, did you hear about the new wing they're building onto the high school? I can't believe how this area has grown."

"Yeah," said Tom, trying to keep the conversation going and away from me and baby talk. "And our taxes keep going up. Unlike some school districts, we have very little industry to support us."

Thank God the school expansion became the topic of conversation. I excused myself and went to the bathroom. My face felt like it was on fire and I needed to splash some cool water on my cheeks.

I was standing at the sink when Sue walked in. "Me and my big mouth. I'm sorry, Gina. It just came out."

"Don't worry about it. It was bound to sooner or later. I just wish it had been later after I was pregnant. What if it doesn't take?"

Sue hugged me. "It will. You just have to believe. And you'll be the best mommy ever."

****

Mike

I choked on my steak when Sue spit out the news about Gina having a baby. It didn't surprise me that Gina wanted a baby. She always wanted kids. And Gina wasn't the type of girl who'd let not being married stop her from becoming a mother. When Gina made up her mind to do something, she usually did it. But I wondered about the whole sperm thing. Like how it all worked. Did she get to pick the sperm? Or did she get what she got? I made a mental note to research the process online. I had never thought about it before, but now I was curious.

When we were in high school, we talked about what we thought our lives would be like. If things would have rolled the way we both had planned, our kids would be in junior high by now. I couldn't imagine having a newborn at my age. When Lisa and I split, I figured that Jack would be my only kid. He's a great kid and all that I've ever wanted so I'm cool with that. I had thought about having a vasectomy, especially after someone I hooked up with for a while thought she was pregnant. I was so relieved that it turned out to be a false alarm. She broke it off soon afterward. Guess she figured that if she ended up pregnant, she didn't want it to be to me. I was fine with that. It wasn't like the sex was great anyway. We were both just lonely.

When Gina and Sue returned from the bathroom, Gina's face didn't look as red.

"Everything OK?" Tom asked.

The girls nodded.

"Here comes dessert," Jeremy said. "And it looks delicious."

The waitress set a plate of bananas foster in front of each of us.

Sue licked her lips. "One of my favorites."

"I don't even want to know how many calories are in this," Gina said.

"You look great," Tom said. "A little bit of ice cream, brown sugar, butter, rum and banana liqueur won't hurt you at all."

"It really has all that in it?" Gina asked.

Sue waved her hand. "Oh, who cares? This is one night when we're not going to worry about our figures. Eat up, girlfriend."

"Do you remember the time, Mike," Jeremy laughed, "that you put a banana down your pants and walked up to the Palma-nator. It looked like you had one hell of a hard-on."

Everyone laughed.

I nodded. "It was one of my finer moments. Especially when she suggested that I should perhaps go to the bathroom and I reached down and pulled out the banana, peeled it and took a bite."

"Then she sent you to the principal's office," Gina said. "I remember that because you were grounded and we couldn't go out."

Gina bit her bottom lip. I had forgotten that quirk of hers and how sexy I thought she looked when she did it. I asked her about it once and she had no idea what I was talking about. She never realized that she did it.

For a few minutes, it seemed like old times. Like we were back in high school, just kids flexing our muscles and ready to take on the world. Not nearly 40-year-olds with mortgages and a slew of bills that come faster than the income to pay them. How does it happen? One day you look in the mirror and you're a pimply-faced teen with braces and the next day you're an adult with gray hair, wrinkles and a crown or two. It's a bitch getting older. My back tells me that every day. I know that I'm not as young as I used to be, but I don't feel old. I still feel like that pimply 17-year-old who couldn't put a condom on gracefully if it killed me. Thank God I had Gina. She took care of that.

Chapter 11

Gina

"While you're finishing your dessert, we have some prizes we'd like to give out," Lynn announced. "The first one goes to the classmate with the oldest child. And the winner is Karen Hollinger."

Woots and applause echoed throughout the ballroom. "It just so happens," Cookie continued, "that Karen also has the youngest child, a 14-month-old. So this prize is for both."

Karen walked up to get the black bag with orange tissue paper peeking out of the top.

"And the award for the most kids goes to Keith Oberlander. Keith has five kids, two sets of twin girls and a boy."

The crowd roared.

"I can't imagine five kids," Sue said. "I couldn't handle five Chloes!"

"The next award," Lynn said, "Goes to the classmate who traveled the farthest. And it goes to Gina McKenzie."

Jeremy started pumping his arms. "Woot! Woot! Woot! Woot!"

I bowed my head, trying to avoid the stares. "This is sooo embarrassing."

"Go get your bag," Sue said. "Maybe there's something good in it. Like a chocolate bar or something."

I pushed out my chair and walked up and got the bag from Lynn.

Lynn gave out some more prizes and then the DJ started playing songs.

First up was Survivor's "Eye of the Tiger."

"Come on, Gina," Sue said. "Let's dance."

I shook my head. "Not me. I haven't danced in years."

"You two always had the moves in high school," Jeremy said. "I'm sure you still got them. Teresa will come with you."

Teresa elbowed him in his side.

"Yeah," Mike said. "We'll watch."

I looked at Teresa. "I'll come if Teresa will."

Teresa waved her hand. "I can't dance."

"Sure you can," Jeremy said. "You dance at home."

"That's different."

"True, there's no pole here," Jeremy teased. "And you guys should see what she can do with a pole."

Teresa hit him again and the guys laughed.

Sue came over and pulled me up off my chair and then walked over to Teresa and pulled her off her chair. We took off for the crowded dance floor and shuffled into the sea of people.

I leaned over to Teresa. "Do you really have a pole?"

She nodded. "It's in our bedroom. I use it to exercise, although I have to admit that exercising on the pole usually ends with us exercising on the floor."

I laughed. One guy I dated wanted me to pole dance. I opted for a chair. It was a little easier. I watched Sue as she took command of her space. Sue was always more confident on the dance floor than I was and twenty years hadn't made any difference. Like Jeremy said, she still had the moves.

"Loosen up, girls," Sue yelled to Teresa and me. Her arms flew every which way. "Close your eyes and feel the music."

I tried closing my eyes, but it just made me dizzy. Thank God the song ended and I made a beeline for the table. Sue and Teresa stayed on the dance floor for the next song.

****

140

Mike

"Man, guys," Jeremy said. "Are Sue and Gina still hot or what?"

I nodded. "Yeah. Hot. Very hot. But you're a lucky guy. Teresa's hot and she pole dances."

Jeremy smiled. "Yeah, and it makes me want to fuck her hard every time."

Jeremy looked at Tom. "What about you, Tom? You and Sue would make a good couple. You ought to ask her out. She's not seeing anyone."

"I'd like to, but not sure she'd go out with me."

"Won't know if you don't ask," Jeremy said. "And you, Mike. You've been pining after Gina for twenty years. Christ, you finally end up sitting next to her. If you don't ask her out I'm going to nail you. This is the chance you've been waiting for."

Jeremy was right. I never shook Gina. She was like a tattoo that you can never totally get rid up. The memories might fade and the lines might blur, but my love for her was inked in my soul forever.

Sometimes, I wonder if my memories of Gina and me are too good, if I'm remembering things how I want to remember them, and not how they really were.

I looked toward the dance floor. From the way Sue's body twisted, she looked like she was having a great time. Gina and Teresa? Not so much so. It didn't surprise me that when the music stopped Gina sprinted back to the table.

"Back so soon?" Tom asked.

"I'm too old to move like that."

"You looked like you were moving just fine," Tom said.

"I agree. You held your own out there."

Gina looked at me and rolled her eyes. "Thanks."

When I heard the first few chords of the next song, a lump formed in my throat. It was Willie Nelson's "You Were Always on my Mind." The song came out in the spring of our senior year and, while country wasn't my thing, Gina loved this song. We always slow danced to it.

I glanced over at Gina and her head was bent down. I wondered if she wanted to dance and if I should ask her. My palms felt sweaty. Jeremy went to the dance floor to get Teresa and Tom stood, ready to ask Sue to dance when she returned to the table.

****

Gina

Damn, I love this Willie Nelson song. When we were in high school, I always made Mike dance to this song, even though he hated country. I wondered if he remembered. I didn't want to look at him so I looked down at the table. It's weird how you hear a song that speaks to you at that moment. Sort of like being in church and feeling like the pastor's sermon is just for you.

I felt Mike lean over.

"Would you like to dance?" he asked.

I looked into his dark eyes, and I'm not sure what came over me. Maybe it was the booze or the sweet memories that flooded my mind and filled me with a desire I hadn't felt in years. But I nodded. I wanted to dance.

Mike pulled out my chair and followed me to the dance floor. So many nights I dreamed about being in his arms once again, and here I was. I went to put my hands on his shoulders and pulled them back. I think he could sense I was nervous. He reached down and took my hands and placed them on his shoulders, never taking his eyes off of mine. Then he put his hands on my hips. Still looking into my eyes. I jumped slightly and a smile slid onto his face. Back in the day, my head would have rested on his broad shoulder and his arms would have been wrapped tightly around me.

I smelled his familiar, earthy aftershave. I picked up my foot and stepped on his. "Sorry," I whispered. "Out of practice."

We started to move and I felt the cold fortress I had built to protect myself over the years beginning to melt. It was as if Mike was the sun and I was the earth during the hottest part of the day. Until that moment, I never realized how craved I had been for his touch, how much I longed to bathe in his rays. I didn't want this sun to set – ever. But I knew that the darkness would come – it always does.

I caught Sue and Tom dancing out of the corner of my eye. They seemed to be getting along. Jeremy and Teresa were in front of us. They danced so closely that it was almost obscene. I was glad I wasn't that close to Mike because I'm sure he would have felt my pounding heart. It had been beating on overdrive since he leaned over and asked me to dance. I couldn't believe he still made me feel this way, and I realized that part of the reason I never found anyone is that I had always compared them to Mike. No one ever made me feel the way he had.

I know I was only seventeen, and I've asked myself time and again how someone so young could love so deeply. But I did. And because I did, I broke it off. I loved Mike too much to hurt him and not give him what he needed. And, at that time, I was too broken to do that. It would take years of therapy before I would be able to overcome that.

When the song ended, the DJ played another slow song.

"Wanna stay out here?" Mike asked.

I shrugged my shoulders. "I'm game if you are, unless you want to dance with someone else."

The song was Foreigner's "I've Been Waiting for a Girl Like You."

Oh, great. Another perfect song moment.

****

Mike

When Foreigner came on, I thought, "Oh Christ. This song says exactly how I feel." Creepy how that happens. Only I've been waiting for Gina to come *back* into my life. As we danced, Gina's hair caught the ballroom lights in such a way that it looked like dancing fireflies. So beautiful.

I started to get a pain in my crotch. A grown man getting a hard-on while dancing. God, I'm pitiful. Reminded me of the time in junior high I slow danced for the first time and felt my cock pop. This girl and I were dancing so close that I'm pretty sure she felt it, too. I saw her and her friends giggling afterward so I was pretty sure she had told them. I didn't dance the rest of the night.

I'm sure not having sex for a while wasn't helping things now. The last time was probably a year ago and I came so fast the woman called me "Minute Man." She was pissed, and I think it was the last time we hooked up.

I was glad when the song ended and the tempo picked up with John Mellencamp's "Jack and Diane."

We were the last ones to get back to the table. After I sat down, I reached under the tablecloth and repositioned my penis through my pants. I felt like such a kid.

"Who's ready for another round?" Tom asked.

I stood. "I'll come with you. Gina, want another glass of wine?"

She shook her head. "This time, a Miller Lite."

The guys headed to the bar and Teresa excused herself to go to the rest room.

****

Gina

Sue shook her hands. "Oh. My. God. Tom is such a good dancer.

I smiled. "You guys looked great. So, are you going to go out with him?"

"He hasn't asked me out."

"Yet," I said.

"Did he say anything else about me when you talked?" Sue asked.

"No, most of our conversation was actually about the rape."

Sue's eyes popped. "What? Tom knew what that bastard did and didn't tell anyone?"

"Calm down," I whispered and quickly explained to Sue about what happened that night between Tom and Smith after I left.

"So that's how Coach Smith got the black eye?" Sue asked.

I nodded.

"I remember we teased him in class about his wife giving it to him," Sue said."Turns out it was Tom."

"Yeah, Tom said he nailed him good. Said he told Smith that if he ever laid another hand on me, he would kill him."

Sue's eyes flicked up and down. "Oh. I'm liking Tom more and more. Manly man."

Sue looked up. "Ssh! Here they come. And Teresa, too."

When the others got back to the table, the night was winding down. There was more chatter about everyone's kids and how the world is so different from when we were growing up.

"Anyone want to continue this party at our house?" Jeremy said. "Like old times. The kids are at grandma's, so no problem there."

"Sure, why not," Sue said. "You'll come, too, Gina, right?"

"I don't know. I'm tired."

"Oh come on, party pooper. When's the next time you're going to be in town?" Sue asked`.

"I plan on being home in July."

"That's a couple of months from now. Come on, please?"

The idea of going to Jeremy's, who lived in the house he grew up in, was a little too much for me. I have so many memories of being there with Mike. The night was just moving a little too fast for me, and I needed to brake. I didn't like the way I was feeling. I wasn't used to being out of control when it came to my feelings. Usually I could maintain control. But when it came to Mike, I lost it. God, just being near him made me want to feel the incredible orgasms I used to have. When he would be so deep inside of me and then pull out and play with me until I couldn't take it anymore and would grab his back and push him down and deep.

I could tell Sue was a little tipsy. "I don't think you should drive."

"I'll drive her," Tom offered.

I looked at Tom. "Are you sure?"

"Yeah, we'll go to Jeremy's and then I'll make sure she gets home."

Jeremy and Teresa were already walking away from the table.

Tom came over to me. "Don't worry. Besides, you and Mike should talk."

I could tell by the puzzled look on Mike's face that he wondered what Tom had just said to me. After Tom and Sue left, I walked out to the parking lot with Mike. I pulled a pack of orange gum out of my purse. "What a piece?"

Mike smiled. "You still chew that stuff?"

I popped a piece in my mouth. "Yep, hooked for life, I guess."

Mike popped the piece I gave him into his mouth.

"So, did you have a good time tonight?" I asked.

"Yeah. I'm glad I came. How about you?"

"Me, too."

Before I could stop myself from asking, I blurted out, "Want to come over to Mom's house to talk? She's gone for the weekend."

Mike stared into my eyes. I don't think he was expecting the invitation. And, to be honest, I hadn't expected to extend it. But I wasn't ready for the night to end. Maybe Tom was right. Maybe it was time to tell the truth.

****

Mike

I was surprised when Gina invited me to her mom's house to talk. I wondered if there was something in particular she wanted to talk about.

"I'll follow you," I said.

"Mom doesn't have anything to drink, though. I mean, she has water and soda, but no beer."

I held up my hand. "I've had enough."

Pulling into Gina's driveway took me back twenty years, only then I wasn't driving a Lexus but a rusted brown Chevy sedan.

I took a deep breath and followed Gina inside. Everything looked the same. From the hallway, I looked into the living room. Her mom still had the brown plaid sofa and chair she had when Gina and I were dating. Even the tan vinyl ottoman looked like the same one. My eyes lingered on the sofa. I wondered if it still held my secret. I hadn't thought about it in a long time.

I followed Gina back the hallway to the kitchen, stopping to look at the photos hanging on the wall. A lot of these were the same, too. But some had been added, like Gina's college graduation photo and another from law school. I stopped in front of her high school photo. She looked just as beautiful today as she did then. The years had been good to her. At our high school, the girls had to wear a black drape for the "official" yearbook photo, but many, like Gina, got pictures taken by other photographers on their own to give out to friends. Gina's mom had an eight-by-ten of each. In the more casual photo, Gina was peeking through a tree where its trunk split into a V. Her red hair tumbled softly to her shoulders and her emerald eyes were sexy yet innocent, a contradiction like Gina. But it was her smile, always her smile that you saw first when you looked at her.

My eyes went back and forth between the two photos. I wasn't sure which I liked best. They both were great for different reasons. In the more formal photo, the silver heart necklace I had given Gina dangled around her creamy neck. I wondered if she still had the necklace. I wanted to ask her but didn't.

Gina turned around. "I looked like such a dork back then."

"No, you looked gorgeous," I said. "Still do."

I could feel myself blush, and I could have kicked myself in the ass for being so forward. The last thing I wanted to do was scare Gina away.

"Thanks," Gina said. "But I'm not that kid anymore."

"None of us are. Although there are times I wish I was."

"Really?"

"Yeah. I mean, we had some good times. No real responsibilities. No bills to pay. Nothing to worry about except getting good grades and staying out of trouble."

Gina laughed. "And we didn't always stay out of trouble, did we?"

"True, but we never did anything really bad. Just the normal teen stuff. Like drinking."

"Speaking of drinking, what would you like? Coffee? Tea? Soda?"

"Coffee sounds good."

I followed Gina into the kitchen. It, too, looked the same with its painted yellow cabinets with black hinges and knobs. I smiled when I saw her mom's red cookie jar. It still sat on the counter by the refrigerator. Her mom always kept it filled with Oreos. I walked over and lifted the lid. I shook my head and smiled.

"She still puts Oreos in there," Gina said. "It's one of the first things I check whenever I visit."

Gina and I always hit her mom's cookie jar after school.

"Some things never change," I said. "And that's a good thing. Some things shouldn't change. They're good just the way they are."

Gina turned the coffee pot on. "Mom's been talking about moving into a condo. She doesn't need this big house and the yard work is too much for her. But she just can't pull herself away from all this." Gina made a windmill motion with her arm.

I pulled out a kitchen chair to sit. "Yeah. It's not easy letting go of the past."

As soon as I said it I could have kicked myself, but it was true and it was how I felt.

"You're right about that," Gina said. "But sometimes we need to let go of the past in order to move on with the future."

Damn. I knew Gina was right and it made me mad that she was always right, but it wasn't what I wanted to hear.

"What about you. Have you let go of the past and moved on?"

"That's sort of what I wanted to talk to you about," Gina said.

If my heart was beating fast before, it was beating warp speed now.

****

Gina

As soon as Mike said it, I figured it was a good segue into what I wanted to tell him. But I wasn't sure where to start. How do you tell someone something that you've spent years trying to forget? And yet, I wondered if it was why I could never really go on with my future the way I had wanted to. It was unfinished business, and I think I always knew that there would come a time when I needed to finish it.

I filled one of Mom's brown stoneware mugs and handed it to Mike. "Room for cream, right?"

Mike smiled. "And Earl Grey for you, right?"

I nodded, grabbed a mug, filled it with water and heated it in the microwave.

I grabbed some Oreos out of the cookie jar and handled a couple to Mike. "For old times' sake."

"I'll eat Oreos anytime," Mike said. "When I buy them, Jack eats the whole bag before I get any. I think he hides them in his room so he doesn't have to share."

I sat across from Mike. "We can go into the living room if you want. Might be more comfortable."

"I'm fine," Mike said. "But if you want to move…"

"No. I'm good here." I took a sip of my tea, trying to muster the courage to say what I needed to say.

"Everything OK, Gina?" Mike asked. "You seem a bit tense. You're biting your lip."

Damn him, I thought. I am tense. Very tense. I touched my lips with my hand.

"Still have that habit, huh?" Mike asked.

I nodded. "Guess so."

"It's OK. I wasn't making fun of you. It's always been something I remembered about you."

I threw back my hair and smiled. "Well, at least you have some good memories of me."

Mike sat up straighter. "Whoa, Gina. I have a ton of great memories of you."

I pulled an Oreo apart. "But some bad ones, right?"

"Well, yeah. Some bad ones, too. But more good than bad."

I didn't take my eyes off of Mike's. "That's kind of what I wanted to talk to you about. The bad memories, or rather, what caused them. There's something I've wanted to tell you. It's, well, it's been on my mind for a long time."

"How long?"

"Like twenty years."

"O-K," Mike said, running his hand through his hair. "What is it that you've waited twenty years to tell me?"

My phone rang. I looked at the caller ID. "It's Mom. She's probably calling to find out how the reunion was. I better take it or she'll worry about me."

"Sure," Mike said. "Want me to go into the living room?"

Gina shook her head. "Hello, Mom. Oh, Judy, it's you. Why are you using Mom's phone?"

"What! Omigod, no! How? What hospital? No. I'm coming. I'll try to get there in four hours. Judy, thanks."

Tears exploded from my eyes and I jumped up from the table. "I gotta go. Mom's in a hospital in New York. Judy said they were getting ready for dinner and she dropped over."

"I'll drive you," Mike said.

"No. I can go myself. Besides, you said you and Jack were going to a baseball game tomorrow."

"I'm sure Jack would understand."

"Thanks," I said. "But I better go alone. Not sure how long I'll be there."

Mike's arms were around me. "OK, but if you need anything, please call."

Mike wrote his number on a piece of paper he found on the counter and handed it to me. "I mean it, Gina. Call me and let me know what's going on. I care."

I took the slip of paper. "Can you see yourself out? I gotta change."

"Sure, no problem," Mike said. "Go change and be careful driving."

****

Mike

I was worried about Gina's mom, but it was killing me that I didn't get to hear what Gina wanted to tell me. Twenty years is a long time to have something on your mind.

I stopped in front of the door and glanced into the living room. My eyes fell on the plaid couch. Gina was still upstairs. I dashed over and unzipped the right couch cushion. I stuck my arm in and waved it from one side to the other. I felt it. After 20 years, it was still there. I didn't take it out. I was afraid Gina would come downstairs and catch me, so I just zipped up the cushion.

As I walked away, the past jerked to the present. Gina and I were watching movies on the plaid couch. She told me she didn't love me anymore, that she had been pretending the whole time because she didn't want to hurt me. I punched the couch and walked out the door. That was the end.

Until now. Twenty fuckin' long years later. Damn, I didn't want this to be the end. Maybe I had another shot. Maybe we had another shot. I couldn't believe how the day had turned out. I couldn't believe that I sat beside Gina at the reunion. Hell, I wasn't even sure she'd talk to me if she came. And we danced and I held her. Christ, I even got a hard on. I felt like a teenager and I didn't want the feeling to go away.

I thought about following her to New York, just in case she needed me. But I was afraid if I pushed too hard too soon, I'd scare her away. And I definitely didn't want to do that. I didn't want to screw up any possible second chance I might have with Gina. So I did the only thing I could do; I went home to an empty house.

****

Gina

I scrambled up the steps taking two at a time. I ditched my clothes and whipped my hair into a ponytail. I washed my face and brushed my teeth and threw on a pair of jeans and my pink Nike sweatshirt. I peeked out my bedroom window and watched as Mike pulled away from the house. I wanted to tell him; I would have told him. But I had to get to Mom. Mike would have to wait. I waited twenty years to tell him, what would a day or two matter? Besides, Judy didn't sound good on the phone. I stuffed some clothes into my gray Coach carry-on and grabbed what I thought I might need. I locked up the house and headed for the highway, going faster than I should have on rain-slick roads.

I hoped to make it to New York in four hours. Normally, it would take closer to five. But with any luck, the traffic would be light given that it was nearly midnight. I just needed to stay awake. I sipped the coffee I had put in one of Mom's travel mugs. I wasn't a big coffee fan, but I knew it would help keep me awake. Besides, I had made a whole pot and it would have taken longer to boil water for tea.

I'm not a praying person, but I prayed over and over. I hoped God was listening and that he wouldn't punish me for my lack of prayers over the years. He probably felt like I only prayed when I needed something. And, to be honest, he would be right. Just got out of the habit, I suppose. Doesn't make it right, but it's the truth.

Chapter 12

Mike

I thought about stopping at Jeremy's on my way home, but decided that by now, they would all be pretty wasted. So I headed home instead.

I hated coming home to an empty house. I liked it much better when Jack was here. He was noisy and messy and didn't always listen, but at least I wasn't alone. Sometimes, I turned on the TV just so there'd be some noise in the house.

Maybe I should get a dog. Not a fluff ball like Lisa has, but a German shepherd or Golden Retriever, the kind of dog that I could wrestle and not be afraid I would crush.

I felt sweaty and jumped in the shower. I closed my eyes and let the water beat down on my face. Christ, I thought. Even after all these years Gina still makes me feel like a horny teenager. I had forgotten how much I loved her smile, the way it slipped onto her face even when she didn't want it to. And her hair, that gorgeous mane of red hair. God, I wanted to bury my face in it. I reach down and started massaging myself, thinking about Gina. I don't remember the last time I came in the shower.

Before I hit the sack, I checked the answering machine. Jack had left a message saying good night. I smiled. Jack was the best thing that ever happened to me, and I wondered if one day Jack would meet Gina and if he did, what he'd think of her.

After Lisa, I vowed I would never marry again. But that was before tonight. Just being close to Gina drove me insane. It was electric. I know she felt it, too. I wanted to hold her like I used to hold her, make her feel the way I used to make her feel. I wanted to watch her come as I called her name and leave her drained and sated. Christ, just thinking about the things I wanted to do for her gave me another hard-on. I was pathetic.

But it was more than just the sex that turned me on about Gina. It was the way she bit her pouty bottom lip. The way she tucked her hair behind her tripled pierced left ear and wrinkled her nose when she didn't like something. Her little quirks that I had fallen in love with so long ago.

I looked at the clock on my nightstand. I figured that Gina would get to New York by four. It was a little after one.

Gina

I was right. There wasn't a lot of traffic on the road. I turned up the radio so it would help keep me awake. Mom had it on a station that played the kind of music you'd hear in a dental office. S-L-O-W. I switched it to a classic rock 'n' roll station.

I remember when my dad died. I was in law school. And, much like tonight, I left college in the middle of the night to meet Mom at the hospital. Dad had a massive stroke, and Mom found him on the couch watching TV. He never recovered.

Mom was a basket case. Turned out, Dad took care of all of the finances. He paid all the bills, knew when the taxes were due and the sewer and water bills. Mom took care of the house, laundry and grocery shopping. And cooking. She was, I mean is, a great cook. I'm not knocking her, but that's the way it was. She was happy to let Dad be in charge of the finances.

Of course, Dad always kidded and said that he was in charge of the big things and Mom was in charge of the little things but that nothing big ever happened.

After he died, I had to teach Mom how to manage the household expenses. At first, she didn't want anything to do with writing out the bills, but I told her that she had to learn, that I wasn't going to be around the rest of her life to take care of everything for her.

I pushed and she pushed back. Eventually, she was handling it all on her own and would get mad if I tried to help. "I can do it by myself," she'd say. Mom became quite independent. I'm sure Dad was turning over in his grave. He had tried to get Mom involved in paying the bills, but she complained so much that he dropped it.

I often wondered what it would have been like if I hadn't been an only child. I was the only one of my friends who didn't have a sibling. I was also the only one who had been adopted.

The things you think about when you're driving alone in the middle of the night on a dark highway headed for the unknown.

I remembered the time I had asked Mom if she minded if I searched for my birth mother. At first, she was scared. She thought that if I found my birth mother that I wouldn't love her anymore. But I told her that she was my mother and would always be my mother. Nothing would ever change that.

I met the woman who gave birth to me in the food court at a mall about two hours from home. It didn't go well, and I wished I hadn't looked her up. She used swear words like I use pronouns. Thank God she didn't have red hair like me. Her hair was a mousy brown, shoulder length and frizzy. She was so thin she looked like if you sneezed you'd blow her away. She chain-smoked during our hour-long visit and her fingers and teeth were stained from the tobacco. I hate smoke, and when I coughed she continued to blow it in my direction.

I cried the whole way home. Mom was waiting up for me, and I knew she couldn't wait to hear how it went. I remember looking into Mom's eyes and telling her that I never wanted to talk about my birth mother again. That she was my mom and no one else. And we hugged a long time, neither one of us wanting to break the embrace.

When I got to the hospital, the emergency room was standing room only. What were all of these people doing in an emergency room at four in the morning? I had to remind myself that I was in New York and not in the small town I grew up in. I searched the crowd but didn't see Judy.

"Excuse me," I said to the receptionist. "I'm here to see my mother. She was brought it several hours ago. Her name is Betty McKenzie."

The nurse checked his computer. "Follow me."

He pushed a big square metal button on the wall and the wide double doors opened. Nurses and doctors buzzed about with charts and portable monitors. Everyone seemed in a hurry. I followed the nurse down the hall to the last door on the right. He opened the door and I walked in to find Judy and a pastor.

Judy stood up and held out her arms. Her face was blotchy and red.

I ran and hugged her.

"I'm so sorry," she cried. "I tried to save her. Gave her CPR but it was no use."

"No," I shook my head. "She's not dead. She can't be gone."

"It all happened so fast," Judy continued. "She was fine all day and then when we were getting ready to go out for dinner, she just fell over."

I couldn't keep the tears from pouring out of my eyes. Mom was all I had left. We didn't have a big family. There were no aunts and uncles, on either side and my grandparents were long gone. It was just Mom and me. And now I was alone.

The pastor stood. "I'm Pastor Paul. I'm one of the hospital chaplains."

He shook my hand. "I'm here if you want to talk."

"Can I see her? I want to see her," I said.

The pastor left the room to find someone to help. I sat beside Judy on the vinyl couch. She slipped her arm around me. "We were having such a great time," said Judy, blowing her nose. "We went to a matinee and shopped. I just can't believe she's gone. She loved you, Gina. You were everything to her. She was so happy she was going to be a grandma."

I looked up at Judy. "She told you about that?"

"She told the entire card club about it. We were supposed to pray for good sperm," Judy laughed.

I couldn't keep from laughing either. "That's my mom."

The pastor returned with a nurse. I looked at Judy. "Do you want to come?"

Judy started crying hard again. "You go. I've already said what I needed to say."

163

"Would you like me to come along?" Pastor Paul asked.

I shook my head. "God never seems to listen to my prayers," I said, and followed the nurse out the door.

I pulled back the white cotton sheet covering Mom and felt her arm. "She's cold," I cried. "Can't we get her some blankets?"

The nurse who had brought me back placed his hand on my shoulder. "Your mother is in a better place now."

"Screw that," I said. "I don't want her in a better place, I want her here. With me. She's supposed to be here with me."

I pushed the chair across the room next to the hospital bed. I sank down in the chair and took Mom's hand in mine. I put my head down on the edge of the mattress and cried. It was so unfair, I thought. Now it was just me. I had never felt more alone in all my life.

I made arrangements to have Mom's body transferred to the funeral home that we used when my dad died. Mom liked the funeral director there and said more than once that whenever it was her time to go, she wanted Dan to be the one to take care of things.

Judy rode home with me instead of going home on the tour bus. We cried most of the way. She called some of mom's friends on the way home and I called Sue, getting her out of bed. I also called and left a message at work that I would be out at least a week, maybe longer. Just thinking about everything I had to do made my head spin.

"You know what your mom would say," Judy said. "Take one step at a time. And the first one is getting through the funeral."

"I know you're right, Judy. But there's just so much to do. And it's only me."

"Oh, Gina. You know that I'll help you in any way I can. Just let me know what you need me to do."

"I know, Judy. It's not like I thought you wouldn't help. But, you know, I don't have any siblings to share this with. It's a lot to handle alone."

"My sweet child," Judy said. "You're not alone. You have me. And Sue. You know Sue will help."

I nodded. "I'm pretty sure Mom had everything written down."

"Well, I know she wanted a Lutheran church service," Judy said.

"With Communion," I added, smiling.

"And I know the hymns she liked," Judy said.

I patted Judy's hand. "She showed me once where she kept a list of things she wanted at her funeral. It included hymns and the flowers that she wanted. It's in her underwear drawer in a manila envelope marked 'My funeral' in black marker."

"That's your mom. Always prepared. Funny, I was the one with all of the health problems. Never thought she'd be gone before ..."

Judy started crying again. "Remember that time she ran out of gas when you were little and the car just plain stopped?"

I laughed. "I remembered. She couldn't figure out what was wrong with the car. Turned out, it just needed gas."

We laughed.

"Or the time she forgot to put up the garage door and backed into it when she went to pull out?"

"Oh yeah. I've never seen Dad so mad. His face turned purple and words came out of his mouth I didn't even know he knew."

It felt good to remember and laugh. And cry.

I dropped Judy off at her house and when I finally pulled into Mom's driveway I felt like I'd been through a war. Sue was waiting for me when I walked into the house. She hugged me so tightly it made me cough.

"I'm so sorry, Gina. I loved your mom. She was one of the loveliest people I know."

I broke down and Sue walked me into the kitchen. I smelled fresh-brewed coffee and couldn't help but smile when I noticed my favorite blueberry bagels and a box of Earl Grey on the kitchen table.

"The coffee's for me," Sue said. She picked up the box of Earl Grey. "And I stopped and got tea just in case your mom was all out."

I dabbed my tired eyes with tissues. "You're an amazing friend. Thanks for coming."

"Well of course I'd come. I might still be nursing a hangover from last night, but that's nothing compared to what you're dealing with."

I smiled. "That's right. Last night. You have to tell me all about it. And I want every detail. Don't let anything out."

"Later. We'll talk about that later. Let's talk about your mom now."

I poured a cup of hot water from the white Corning ware tea kettle sitting on top of the stove. Holding the kettle with the blue cornflower on the side warmed me in a strange way. I must have boiled hundreds of cups of water using this kettle over the years.

I turned around and pulled out a chair, unwrapping a tea bag and dunking it in my mug. "Did you find the envelope?"

Sue nodded. "It was right where you said it would be -- in her lingerie drawer. I've already called the minister and he's getting the word out. He said he will be over later. Oh, and the funeral director called and I told him that we would meet with him tomorrow morning."

"We?"

"Yes, we. I'm not going to let you go through this alone. Besides, she was like a mom to me, too."

I hugged Sue tightly. She was an awesome friend, and I was so glad that after all these years, our friendship had remained strong. No matter

167

where our lives had taken us, we were always there for each other.

****

Mike

The light on the answering machine was blinking when Jack and I got home from the baseball game.

I pressed the play button. "Mike, it's Jeremy. I was just calling to let you know that Gina's mom died. Sue called this morning and asked me to let you know. Anyway, talk to you later."

I slapped the desk. "Damn!"

"Is that hot Gina from high school?" asked Jack, taking the lid off the gallon of double chocolate chip ice cream we bought on the way home.

"I never said she was hot," I corrected him. "I said she was pretty."

Jack shrugged. "Same difference. Did you see her at your reunion?"

"You sure ask a lot of questions, kiddo."

"So what's the answer, Dad? Dance or no dance?"

I cleared my throat. "Yes, I danced with her. All right?"

"Did you like it?"

"Yes, it was fun dancing with her. Now enough with the questions."

"Mom says that I should be a reporter because I ask so many questions."

"And she's right. You'd make a great reporter. You're nosey enough to be one."

I told Jack I was going to hit the shower while he finished eating his ice cream. By the rate he was going, that gallon would be polished off by morning. I promised I'd help him study for his spelling test. He hated Mondays as much as I did.

****

I had been thinking about Gina all day. I wasn't prepared to feel the way she made me feel. It had been so long since we'd been together and our lives were now worlds apart. I went to the reunion hoping that if I saw her, we'd be able to be friends. But dancing with her, smelling that sexy Gina smell, made me want so much more. All of those old desires came rushing back and knocked me over.

I had no idea what Gina wanted to tell me, and just thinking that it was something she's wanted to tell me for twenty years was driving me crazy. What could be that important? I knew that whatever it was, it made Gina nervous. I could tell by the way her leg shook. It's her nervous twitch. And, to be honest, I was a bit scared to find out. I figured it had to do with me, otherwise she wouldn't be telling me it. And it scared me to think of the possibilities.

It's no secret Gina broke my heart. I was so depressed my first semester in college that I damn near flunked out. I finally came around, but not before doing some major damage to my GPA. I ended up writing a letter to the head of the engineering department begging for a second chance. When he asked me why my grades sucked, I was completely honest with him. I figured I had nothing to lose. That was the day he looked me square in the eyes and told me that he was going to give me a second chance, but that I better hadn't disappoint him. That if he was going to give me a chance, I had to live up to my end of the bargain. It was either that or find another major.

I stepped it up and recovered – with the help of some great tutors that cost me a bundle. But it was worth every penny.

****

Gina

Sue woke me when Pastor Greg arrived. I had taken a nap after Sue insisted I try to get some sleep. I hadn't seen Pastor Greg in years, but I never forgot his wilderness sermon. I felt like I was in the wilderness again – although a very different wilderness than the one I fought so many years to make it out of. When I came downstairs, Sue and Pastor Greg were deep in conversation.

Pastor Greg stood when he saw me and held out his hand. "Nice to see you again, Gina. Although I wish it was under other circumstances. I'm so sorry. Your mom was a wonderful woman."

I nodded and half smiled. "Yes, she was."

I handed him the envelope. "Mom wrote it all down. She wants a full Lutheran church service and she has a list of hymns she liked the organist to play."

Pastor Greg opened the envelope and took out the piece of paper. He smiled. "Looks like it's all here. What about after the service? The ladies in the church can provide a meal. Your mom always helped with the funeral dinners; I know they would like to do this for her."

"That's fine," I said. "Just let me know what it cost."

"Most of it will be donated," Pastor Greg said. "There will be little cost."

We talked about Mom for a little bit and after a prayer, Pastor Greg left.

I looked over at Sue, who was knitting. "Do you believe in God?"

Sue put down her needles. "Yeah, don't you?"

"I guess so. I just don't understand why bad things happen to good people. Like why little kids who haven't hurt anyone or done anything wrong get cancer and die."

"Most people wonder that," Sue said. "Mom always said that everything happens for a reason, we just don't always see it right away."

I bit my bottom lip. I wasn't going to say it but I couldn't help myself. "What about me? Why did I get raped?"

"Oh, Gina," said Sue, putting down her knitting needles and walking over me. "I don't know why something so terrible happened to you. And I haven't been able to get it out of my mind since you told me. And, I'm still mad that you kept this to yourself all of these years. And as horrible as it was, it is, look what you've accomplished with your life? You've helped lots of women who were in your situation get justice. Maybe that's why it happened, as twisted as it sounds. I mean, I'm not sure you would have become a lawyer prosecuting sex crimes if it had not been for your past. I always wondered where your passion for this area of law came from. It's all so clear to me now. Look how many people you've helped. How many bastards you put in jail."

I started to cry. I couldn't help it. Mom dying and finally telling Sue about the rape and my decision to tell Mike boiled into a crying mess.

Sue stroked my hair. "Remember, one day at a time."

"More like one hour at a time," I said.

"Whatever works," Sue said. "Reminds me of that one Christmas show we always used to watch. You know the one with the Burgermeister and the Winter Warlock."

I knew exactly which one she was talking about. It was from "Santa Claus is Coming to Town." We broke out in song, "just put one foot in front of the other. And soon you'll be walking cross the floor."

We laughed. Sue always made me laugh. It was one of the things I loved most about her.

****

I stood in front of the red brick funeral home on Main Street, across from the Lutheran church I grew up in. I could feel my entire body tense up, like a twisting rubber band. Let go and I would snap and unravel. I rubbed the muscle in my neck. It felt like a big sailor's knot.

I didn't want to meet with the director. I didn't want to pick out the casket. When Dad died a few years back, I helped Mom with the funeral details. I tried to be strong for Mom, but deep down I hated it. And I knew that I never wanted to pick out a casket ever again. And here I was. Damn, I hated life sometimes.

Sue took my hand. "It'll be all right. I'm here with you. We can do this together."

Her words, her friendship turned me into a sobbing mess. Together, we walked through the massive carved oak door with a floral arch.

Mr. Little showed us the caskets. Tears pooled in my eyes. I looked away. "I'm not sure I can do this again."

"How about this one," Sue said. "Your mom loved mahogany. Her bedroom set is mahogany. This is beautiful."

I glanced over at Sue. She was standing next to the casket. It was beautiful. Well, as beautiful as a casket can be.

"It has antique hardware," Mr. Little explained. "And an adjustable bed and mattress."

Christ, I thought to myself, he's talking about it like it's a damn bed. "That one's good. Can we get out of here?"

I caught the arched-eyebrow look Mr. Little flashed Sue. She nodded to him and we followed him to his office down the hall.

He opened a desk drawer and pulled out about a dozen funeral cards with various designs. He fanned them out on the desk in front of us. I took a deep breath.

Sue immediately pulled one out. "Oh, look, Gina. Your mom loved the Footprints in the Sand poem. This one's perfect."

Sue was right. The front had "In loving memory" on top of footprints in the sand. Inside was the poem and space to add the personal details. I nodded and Mr. Little put the others away.

"Is this memorial registry book OK?" He held up a white, hardbound leather book.

"Sure. It's fine. All of this is just fuckin' fine."

I ran out the door, and I heard Sue tell Mr. Little that if he needed to know anything else, he should call her.

I ran out the door and across the street to a small park and sat on a bench. Sue sat down beside me and put her arm around me. "I'm sorry, Gina."

I couldn't contain the volcano of tears any longer. They spewed out of me like they had been pent up and bubbling forever. "She won't be here to see me have my baby. She was supposed to help me. Not leave me. Now I have no one left."

"You have me," said Sue, brushing back my hair.

"You know what I mean. You have brothers and sisters and aunts and uncles. It's always just been me and mom and dad. I feel so all alone."

"Families aren't always blood related," Sue said. "You know that better than anyone. Chloe and I will always be your family."

I buried my head in Sue's shoulder and cried for what seemed like hours. "Thank you for coming with me today."

"I wouldn't have had it any other way. Ready to go home?"

I nodded. "I guess I have to go home sometime, huh?"

Sue nodded. "Do you want me to stay over tonight?"

"No. I'll be fine. You've done so much already. I plan to go to bed early, and I think I'd rather just be alone, if you don't mind."

Sue pulled up to the curb. "Sure you're going to be all right?"

I nodded.

"If you get hungry, there's food in the refrigerator that the ladies at the church dropped off earlier. It was a lot, so I stuck some of it in the freezer.

"Thanks." I opened the door. "See you later, Tig."

Sue laughed. "No one's called me that in ages."

"Well," I said. "I'm feeling a bit nostalgic and a bit like Eeyore. And I need your bouncing Tigger self to keep me afloat."

Sue laughed. "See you later, Gina. Remember. Call if you need anything."

****

Opening the front door jolted me back to when I was in school. I remember coming home and Mom calling my name from the kitchen when she heard the front door close. She'd be peeling potatoes or rolling out potpie dough or making one of her yummy apple pies or a batch of soft sugar cakes. The sugar cakes were my favorite, and it occurred to me that I never asked her for the recipe, that I never actually made them myself. It was something that Mom always made, something I looked forward to eating every time I came home to visit.

I checked the answering machine. There was a call from Judy, but I didn't feel much like talking. Instead, I headed to the bathroom for a lavender soak. Mom always kept a bottle of bubble bath on hand for those times when the only thing that soothed you was a long soak in the tub.

I drew the bath water and crawled in, slipping completely under with only my head above water. I closed my eyes as the warm water embraced me in a gentle stillness. When I opened my eyes, my skin was red and wrinkled. And the water was cold.

****

Mike

Jack was spending the night at Lisa's house. It was his step-dad's birthday and Lisa was throwing a big bash. Jack had called earlier and said Lisa had hired caterers to take care of all of the details and that the food was "out of this world." He sounded like he was having a good time.

I couldn't get Gina off my mind. Even taking a shower didn't help. I wondered if she was OK. A part of me wanted to drive over and find out, but another part of me thought that I might get the door slammed in my face. I threw a frozen chicken dinner into the microwave and followed that up with a peanut butter sandwich, and then a banana.

I tried watching TV, but it was no use. I couldn't stop thinking about Gina. Damn. That's it. I grabbed my keys and wallet off of the kitchen table and drove over to her house. I thought maybe Sue would be there, but I didn't see her car. I waited in my car, trying to get up the nerve to go to the door. I hit the steering wheel with the palm of my hand. What the hell. I have nothing to lose. I went to the door and knocked. I waited a few more minutes and knocked again.

"I'm coming," I heard Gina say.

When she opened the door, she looked like she had just crawled out of the shower. Her head was wet and she looked like a kid in an oversized plaid shirt that looked like it had belonged to her father.

"I told you I'd be OK" Gina said as she opened the door.

She jerked back. "Oh, Mike. It's you. I thought it was Sue."

"Can I come in?" I asked. "I was worried about you. I wanted to make sure you were OK."

"So you heard?"

I nodded. "Jeremy called."

Gina started to cry and I put my arms around her and led her to the couch.

"First Dad; now Mom," Gina exploded. "There's no one left."

"Gina, you have friends. Like Sue. And I'd like to be your friend, if you'll let me."

Gina blew her nose. "This house. What am I supposed to do with this big, old house. And all the stuff? Mom saved everything."

"Look, I'll help. I have a friend who sells houses. If that's what you want to do. Sell it."

Chapter 13

Gina

When I opened the door and saw Mike, I couldn't stop the tears from taking over. It was like everything I had been feeling – the desperation and loneliness and uncertainty – fizzed and blew the lid off my emotions. My whole body wracked with mournful sobs that started way down deep, so deep that by the time they reached the surface their power scared me.

Mike put his arms around me and I felt as though he was pulling me onto a life raft. I felt safe and protected. Maybe even loved.

When he offered to contact one of his friends about the house, my sobs crescendoed. My world had changed tempo overnight and I was thrust into a mournful lament.

"But if you don't want to sell the house, don't," Mike said.

"What would I do with it?"

"Ever think of moving back?" he asked.

"Are you kidding me? I have a great job. To leave everything I've worked so hard for and move back here. Why would I? Especially now that Mom's gone. And Sue and Chloe fly down to see me a few times a year."

As soon as I said it I could see the hurt on Mike's face. His furled brows always gave him away.

"I thought maybe seeing everyone at the reunion might have given you the itch, you know, to move back."

"Seeing everyone also brought back a lot of pain," I said.

"What do you mean pain? Do you mean me?"

His eyes searched mine.

"No. You never caused me pain. You were among the good parts of this place."

"So why'd you dump me?"

I bit my bottom lip. I knew sooner or later it was going to come to this, and I really wasn't up for talking about it.

Mike caught my sigh. "I'm sorry, Gina." He touched my arm. "I didn't mean to go there, especially now."

"That's OK," I said. "I knew you'd ask sooner or later."

"That's what you wanted to talk to me about the other night, wasn't it?" Mike said.

I nodded. "But I'm too tired to go into it right now. Can we talk later? Maybe after the funeral. I need to make it past that."

"Sure. I understand. Need help with anything?"

I shook my head. "I think Sue has everything under control. The ladies at the church are doing the funeral luncheon in the church social hall. Mom would have liked that. She always helped with the funeral luncheons."

Mike looked around the living room. "Do you remember the last time we sat together on this couch?"

I bit the inside of my cheek. "How could I forget?"

"Believe me, I've tried to forget many times," Mike said. "But you don't forget the love of your life breaking up with you."

"Oh, come on," I said. "It wasn't that bad."

"It was, too," Mike said. "Damn near made me want to become a priest."

We both laughed. "Somehow I can't see you being a priest."

"Guess I would have an awful lot of things to repent for."

"No more than the rest of us," I said. "Well, most of the rest of us."

****

Mike

I love hearing Gina's bubbly laugh. She's right. I wasn't priest material.

"In all seriousness, I can't believe twenty years have passed since BMH day," I told her.

"BMH day?" Gina asked.

"Yeah. The day you Broke My Heart."

Gina playfully hit my arm. "A lot's happened in those twenty years."

"Yep," I agreed. "A lot's gone down. But some things haven't changed."

"Like what," Gina asked.

"Like how beautiful you are."

Gina blushed red tulips. "Oh, come on. Guess you haven't noticed the wrinkles hugging my eyes."

I smiled. "Those?" I touched the corner of her eyes. "They're laugh lines. They add character."

"Character, huh? You always were a smooth talker."

"When it came to you, I always told the truth. There was never any bullshit. It's still that way. You breaking up with me really pissed me off, especially since I had no idea what I did wrong."

"Stop," Gina said. "Not now. No talking about that now."

I ran my fingers through my hair. "Jesus, Gina. You're more beautiful than I remembered."

"Even with no makeup on?"

I touched her cheek. "You've never needed makeup."

Gina looked down. "Thanks. I haven't felt beautiful in a long time."

I lifted her chin and stared into her green eyes. "You're more beautiful than you've ever been."

I couldn't help myself. I had to kiss her. I had to feel her silky skin next to mine. I ached to hold her in my arms, to kiss her everywhere. It was all I could do to hold myself back. It's was like seeing an opening during a basketball game and wanting to run through it and make a basket. Only I didn't want to screw up and miss. Oh, what the hell. I went for the shot.

****

Gina

When our lips touched, I felt things I hadn't felt in 20 years. My body tingled. I wanted him to touch me, undress me, and make love to me. No guy I had ever been with ever made me feel this way. Other than him. I was awakened and suddenly the only thing I could think about was Mike being inside me, making me feel the way I knew I could feel. God, I missed that.

I felt like I was at the edge of a cliff. I knew that if I jumped I could land on jagged rocks below, but I didn't give a damn. I jumped. Fast. I wanted more. I needed more. I needed Mike. I wanted to feel him inside of me. I wanted him to take me. I unbuttoned his shirt and planted a trail of kisses down his chest. He moaned as I reached for the top of his jeans and ran my hand over his bulging crotch.

Mike pulled back. "Gina, you're driving me crazy. Are you sure? I don't want to hurt you."

I answered by pulling his head toward mine and kissing him hard and deep. He tasted good. Sweet. God how I missed that sweetness.

He pulled back again. "Not here. I want you to be comfortable."

"I am comfortable," I said, slipping off my oversized shirt and exposing my breasts.

"Oh, Gina, baby." Mike's mouth found one breast and I moaned as he kissed and sucked while rolling the other nipple between his two fingers. My nipples hardened in response and my body felt like it was doing cartwheels. I was head over heels for this man. Still.

And then I felt Mike lift me off the couch. He carried me upstairs to my bedroom, which hadn't changed in twenty years. Cheerleading trophies sat on my white dresser and my porcelain doll collection filled the shelf Dad had built. My violin and music stand were by the window. Everything was the same.

Even this.

Mike laid me down. I pulled him toward me, devouring his mouth with mine once again.

"Oh, God, Gina."

He undressed and lay down beside me, kissing my jaw line, his sweet mouth trailing down to my breasts. Our bodies tangled, rolling one way and then the other. I had never felt such electricity in all my life. It was like twenty years of longing came pouring out in seconds.

Mike was kissing me in places that hadn't been kissed in forever. I felt his hardness on my inner thigh and begged him to enter me.

"You're torturing me," I said. "I can't take it. Please."

"Oh, sweet baby," he moaned and he found his way inside me. I had forgotten how good he felt. He toyed with me, pulling back. I couldn't take it anymore. I grabbed a hold of his back and forced him in as deep as I could. Our bodies fell into sync and just when I thought I couldn't take it anymore, we came together. It was the most incredible feeling in the whole world. I never had sex this good – ever. It was as if our bodies were meant for each other. A perfect fit. I fell asleep, wrapped in his arms.

****

Mike

I kissed the top of Gina's head, cradled in the crook of my arm. Holy Christ. I can't believe what just happened. This woman, this crazy woman that I never stopped loving wanted me. I came so hard and it felt so good. But then I started feeling guilty. I wondered if I had taken advantage of Gina's fragile emotional state. What if she woke up and was pissed and blamed me for us ending up in bed together? But she was the one who forced it when I tried to stop. And her response to me was so strong that it almost bowled me over. Her body beckoned mine.

I brushed her long red hair with my fingers. At that moment, everything seemed perfect. But I knew the moment wouldn't last. Gina would wake up. She had her mom's funeral to get through. She would be selling this house and going back to Florida. And I probably wouldn't see her again until the next class reunion.

I laid there for a long time listening to her breathing. When I woke up, I heard birds chirping outside her bedroom window. I rolled over and saw that Gina was gone.

"Christ," I jumped out of bed. I didn't realize that it was already 6 o'clock. I had to get home, shower and pick Jack up for school before 8. I pulled on my jeans and ran down the stairs pulling my shirt over my head.

Gina was sitting at the kitchen table reading the paper and drinking coffee. Her hair was messy and she was wearing an oversized T-shirt than hung from her shoulders.

"You finally got up," she said.

I walked over and pulled out a chair. "Are you OK?"

Gina smiled. "Yeah, I'm great."

"You're not mad that we, that we, you know…"

Gina smiled. "No. I'm not mad. I'm sorry that I came on so strong last night."

"You were fine. I like strong."

"Well, I'm usually not that pushy."

"Look," I said. "There's no need to explain. I hate to run but I have to go. I need to shower and get ready for work and pick Jack up at 8."

Gina smiled. "No problem."

"Can I see you later?"

"I'm having dinner with Judy."

"How about the next night?"

"The next night is the funeral."

"Oh, yeah. Right."

"But I'll definitely see you before I go back home."

"OK, great," I said. "About last night, though. I hadn't felt that way in a very long time. You're more beautiful than you've ever been. I just wanted you to know that."

Gina smiled and walked me to the door. "Thanks for being here last night. It meant the world to me."

"I've always been here for you, Gina," I said. "You just didn't see me."

****

Gina

Watching Mike drive away left me feeling lonelier than I've felt in a long time. I'm still not sure what came over me last night. It was like my body and my heart were in control and there was no fighting their urges. Feeling Mike deep inside of me, being connected to him so perfectly, took my breath away.

I had been running scenarios over in my mind all morning. Playing the what-if game. What if I moved home? What if I didn't sell Mom's house? What if Mike and I started dating? Oh, that was silly. We screwed. It was just one night. He needed someone and I needed someone and it was all in the timing. It probably didn't mean much to him. I tried lying to myself and telling myself that it was nothing more than a hook-up. But I knew better. I wanted to make love to Mike the moment I saw him at the reunion. And I knew that I would want to make love to him again. But I couldn't let that happen. I was going home. I had cases to prosecute, a life to live. And Mike's life was here, with his son.

I knew that I would have to tell him about the rape before I went home. I wondered how he would take it. Would he be mad? Think that I should have told him when it happened? Understand why I didn't? In my mind, I always rationalized that I didn't lie to Mike I just kept some things from him. But I wondered if he would see it that way. What happened last night made me even more unsure. I don't regret last night. It was the kind of lovemaking that you dream of, soft and tender yet urgent and full of passion.

I filled my mug again with hot water and unwrapped another tea bag. I grabbed Mom's purse off the kitchen counter. I swear the bag weighed fifty pounds. I dumped the contents onto the table.

Lipstick. Checkbook. Pens. Kleenex. Datebook. Wallet. Fingernail file. Sewing kit. Paperback book. New York City map. Photo book. Keys. Brown coat button. Grocery store receipt. Notepad. Tape measure. Band-aids. Chapstick. Sunscreen. Pack of crackers. Gum. Mints. Rolo. Paper clip. Pin.

I picked up the pin and smiled. I had made it for her when I was in elementary school. It was a sun brooch. I had cut a circle out of yellow felt. Using gold glitter glue, I drew a circle in the middle of the felt and rays. Then I finished it by adding a smiley face and a pin to the back. I had no idea Mom had kept this all of these years. It was a little faded. I remember when I gave it to her she said, "I will wear this pin over my heart because that's where I will always carry you."

I reached for the box of tissues. There were so many things I wanted to tell her, so many things I wanted to say, and now I'll never get the chance. We never talked about her dying, other than her telling me about the envelope in her drawer that contained important information.

"Damn you, Mom. Damn you for leaving me."

****

Mike

Driving home, I couldn't get last night out of my mind. When I woke up and Gina wasn't beside me, I thought, *Oh, Christ, is she pissed?* Because I was pumped. Last night was incredible and I was kind of hoping for a repeat in the morning. I couldn't help wanting Gina again. God, this is what she did to me. This is what she always did to me. My groin ached just thinking about her.

When I got home, I jumped in the shower and turned the knob to cold. I grabbed a muffin and nuked a cup of day-old coffee I poured from the carafe. I thumbed through the paper, looking for the obituary. It was at the top of the page. I read through it quickly. *She is survived by a daughter, Gina McKenzie.* A lump formed in my throat. So many times I imagined her name as Gina Parker. I smiled to myself because knowing Gina, she would have wanted to keep her maiden name. That's the way she was. Always wanted her own identity. I remember we got into a big debate one night when we were making out in the woods and talking about the future. Gina said that when we had kids, she wanted to hyphenate their names. I was against that. I told her it was fine to give our kids her maiden name as their middle name, but no hyphen. To be honest, I was kind of hurt by the whole thing. Nothing against having girls, but especially if we would have had a boy. I would want my son to have my last name. Period.

My cell phone rang. It was Jack, calling to remind me to bring his display board for his science project. I was glad he called to remind me because the only thing on my mind this morning was Gina.

Jack opened the car door and slid in. "Got the board?"

I nodded. "It's in the trunk."

"How was the party?"

"Fun. Food was great. Lots of people I didn't know, though."

"How's your mom and the baby?"

"Mom's fine. Paige is her usual annoying crybaby self. I'm never having kids. They cry all the time. You have to feed them and change their diapers. And there's no way I'm wiping someone's butt."

I chuckled. "I wiped your butt. Plenty of times."

"You were stupid," Jack said. "I'm smarter than you."

I smiled. "Guess that means I won't have any grandkids."

Jack nodded. "But you have me and you always say that I'm a lot to handle so grandkids would just be extra work. So I'm saving you extra work."

"Oh, I see." I loved Jack's logic. To him, the world was black and white. And I knew it was so much more.

****

191

Gina

When I picked up the phone and it was Sue I blurted out what happened.

"Oh. My. God." Sue said.

"Yeah, I know. But it just sort of happened."

"Was it good?"

"It was great."

"Now what?"

I knew what Sue was thinking. How was I going to handle things with Mike. "It was only one night. I'll be going back home after the funeral. My life is there and his is here."

"Did you tell him about Coach Smith?"

"Not yet. But I will. After the funeral."

"He's going to be pissed, you know," Sue said.

"On a scale of one to ten, how pissed do you think he'll be?"

"A twelve," Sue said. "Wouldn't you be?"

I took a deep breath. "I wouldn't be pissed as much as I would be relieved that it wasn't me who caused the breakup."

"Oh, sweet Jesus, Gina. Think about it. You broke his heart. Who knows what would have happened if you would have told him the truth."

"But I didn't lie."

"Excuse me? Telling the guy that you didn't love him anymore wasn't the truth."

"That was only so he would accept the breakup."

"Look. I gotta get to work. I'll be over afterward to check on things. I'm sure the talk with Mike will go fine. Love ya."

"Love you, too."

When I hung up the phone I thought about what Sue said. Even if it meant upsetting Mike, I knew I had to tell him the truth. No more lies between us. That's the way it had to be.

I called the office to check in and my secretary, Marcia, told me that she had rescheduled all of my appointments."

"I canceled the one with the fertility specialist," she said. "When do you want me to reschedule that?"

"Give me the number and I'll call and reschedule. The timing's important. I have to check my cycle and figure it out."

"So you're still going to go through with the pregnancy?" Marcia asked.

"Absolutely. I know I won't have Mom to help, but I still want a child. I'll just have to hire a full-time nanny."

"I can help with the hiring," Marcia said. "If you want, I'll screen the candidates first."

"That would be great, Marcia. Anything else?"

"You got a new case. High school math teacher having sex with one of her students. Apparently the kid bragged to some friends and the teacher's been charged. The student's 15. It was in the paper this morning. Made the front page."

"Damn, when are these teachers going to learn," I said.

After I hung up the phone, I called my fertility doctor and we figured out when I should come in for the insemination. My semen had arrived.

****

Mike

It was hard to concentrate at work. I kept thinking about last night and if Gina was OK. She seemed OK this morning, but would that change as the day went on. For me, last night was incredible. Holding her in my arms again. Feeling her soft skin against mine. Touching every inch of her body. Her hair fanning across my chest. Damn, she always did have a way of turning my world upside down.

When my cell rang, I hoped it was Gina. When I saw it was my friend Hillary, I wasn't sure that I wanted to answer. But it was the second time she had called that day. Hill and I were good friends who enjoyed each other's company and occasionally had sex. The sex was always satisfying but that's all it was, sex. We just didn't feel the way about each other that makes sex so much more. There was no way I could think about Hillary now and I knew she probably was horny and wanted to get together. But if I didn't answer, she'd keep calling.

"Hi, Hill. What's up?"

"You free tonight?" she asked.

"No. An old friend's in town and I made some plans with her."

"OK. Call me the next time you're free," she said.

"Will, do."

I seriously hoped that things wouldn't settle down for a long time between me and Gina. I hadn't wanted anyone as much as I wanted her last night. Christ, just thinking about her gave me a hard on. But I didn't want to get my hopes up. After all, Gina's life wasn't here. She'd go back home and I'd stay here.

Damn, Gina and I never seemed to be going in the same direction at the same time. There was always a disconnect, and I doubted that would ever change. But being with her reminded me of how things could be, of what was missing from my life. If I couldn't have it with Gina, maybe I could have it with someone else.

Having sex with Hill was fine, but I wanted more than fine. I wanted to feel as physically close to a woman as I felt to Gina. And I know Gina felt it, too. I could tell by the way her body responded to my touch, the way she raised her hips, begging me to take her away. Feeling her arms around my back pulling me toward her while stealing my breath with her hungry kisses, drove me crazy. I could still smell her lavender skin. God she was good. No great.

Growing old with someone I loved was becoming more important to me. Jack would grow up and hell, who knows where he'd end up. And then I'd be alone – again. Having someone to grow old with sure sounded good. Trouble was, when you've had the best, how do you settle for less? After last night, I wasn't willing to.

Chapter 14

Gina

Sue and Judy stood beside me at the casket, crowded with flowers on either side. A heavy floral scent permeated the air. A line of people snaked through the cavernous room and disappeared around the corner.

I sneezed. I'm not sure why I even bothered to wear makeup. Between the fragrant flowers and my inconsolable grief, I was on my second pack of tissues. I was sure my eyes looked like a panda's.

I knew Mom had a lot of friends, but I didn't expect to see a couple hundred people. Most I hadn't seen in years. I was glad Judy stood beside me because she could tell me who was who. Mom would have felt good that so many people came to say goodbye.

The best part about the evening – if there is a best part – were the stories the older people shared about Mom when she was a young girl. I never knew she was such a mischievous kid. Like the time she hid the tests she found on the teacher's desk. I laughed when Mrs. Snyder told me that story.

I felt as though I got to know Mom better. Sad in a way that it took her funeral to see a side of her I hadn't seen before. To me, she was my mom. But to these people, she was their friend and classmate and Sunday school teacher. It was an exhausting evening, and I knew that tomorrow would be worse.

I remember when Dad died. It was in January, and the day of the burial was biting. Not many people went to the cemetery. It was just too cold. It was just Mom, me, and a few others. At least this time it was April and the weird weather we'd been having made it feel more like summer. I'm sure there'd be a crowd at the burial.

I saw Mike as he turned the corner and entered the room. He looked sharp, dressed in a black suit and white shirt. It took him about an hour to get up to where I stood. As soon as I saw him I broke down. He took me in his arms and whispered in my ear: "So sorry, Gina. If you need anything, I'm here."

I nodded. I wanted to tell him that I needed him. That I was sorry and stupid for ever letting him go. That I missed him already and I just saw him this morning. God, there was so much that I wanted to say but this wasn't the time nor the place. He moved on to Judy, then Sue.

I thought the night would never end. My lower back hurt from standing and my feet were killing me. I should have listened to Sue and skipped the high heels for the pair of flats she offered to let me borrow. I'd wear those tomorrow for sure. All I wanted to do was go home and climb into bed.

When everyone was gone, I leaned over the casket. "I love you, Mom." I patted the sun brooch I had pinned on her coral floral blouse.

She looked so peaceful. Her nails were painted a pale pink and her hands were folded with a red rose stuck in the middle. I picked up the photo of the two of us taken when I was six. I didn't have any front teeth and Mom and I were standing in front of our Christmas tree. I can still picture Dad taking the photo, telling us to make sure the presents we were holding weren't covering our faces. I was holding a purple smiley pillow and Mom was holding a gold bracelet Dad had bought her. Every Christmas, Dad would buy Mom a piece of jewelry. I touched the gold cross that hung down over her blouse and the gold chain bracelet that hugged her sleeve. Gifts from Dad.

She had left instructions that I was supposed to keep her wedding band and engagement ring. Her hope was that I would pass it on if I ever had a child and it would stay in the family.

"Are you ready?" Judy asked, patting me on the back.

I nodded. "Yeah. I'm ready to go home. I mean, to Mom's house."

Judy smiled. "It will always be your home, Gina."

****

Mike

When I left the funeral home, I felt lousy. I don't think I've ever seen Gina so torn up. I wish I could do more for her. I hate funerals. And here I was at my second one in weeks.

I stopped at the old watering hole on Main Street for a beer and burger. I hadn't eaten and there wasn't a whole lot at home to make.

When I walked in, the place was pretty empty. Two tattooed bikers were playing pool in the dimly lit corner. A couple I didn't recognize sat at the one end of the wooden bar. I pulled out a stool at the other end.

"Lager?" Bill the bartender asked.

"Yeah, and a glass of water."

Bill slid the beer in front of me. "Rough day?"

I nodded. "Yeah, rough day all right."

"Anything else?"

"How about a burger, Bill? And some fries."

I sipped my cold draft, thinking about Gina. If someone would have told me a week ago that all of this would happen, I'd have laughed in their face.

By the time my burger and fries arrived, the lager was gone.

Bill nodded. "Another?"

"Yeah, one more."

I bit into my burger when I felt a slap on my back.

"Hey, Mike," Tom said. "Guess we had the same idea."

I turned around and nodded.

Tom sat next to me. "I saw you at the funeral. You were ahead of me. It took me about an hour and half to get through the line."

"Me, too."

"Gina was pretty torn up," Tom said.

"Yeah, I know. I'm not sure I've ever seen her quite like that."

"What can I get you?" Bill asked Tom.

Tom threw his head toward me. "I'll have what he's having. That burger looks good."

I took a swig of my cold draft. "So, did you ask Sue out?"

Tom nodded. "But with everything that's happened, I don't know when that'll be."

"Don't give up on her, Tom. You've waited a long time to ask her out. After Gina's gone, Sue will have time again."

"Do you think she'll go home?"

"Who? Gina? Sure. Of course. Why not?"

Tom shrugged. "I just thought that maybe she might think about moving back."

"I don't think that's gonna happen. Her life's in Florida. Why would she leave a career she worked so hard to build and come back here? And for what?"

Tom shifted in his seat. "You two seemed to be getting along pretty well at the reunion."

"There's a big divide between getting along well and Gina moving here. I just don't see that happening. Unless."

Tom cocked his head to the side and cast an arched eyebrow. "Unless what?"

"Unless she found something that was worth coming back to."

****

The next day was the funeral, and I decided to take a half-day at work and go. Seemed like the right thing to do. I knew Gina hated the cemetery where her Mom would be buried. It was the same cemetery where her friend, Alicia, had been raped. It happened ten or fifteen years ago. Sort of lost track of the time.

Anyway, Alicia had been running through the secluded cemetery at dusk one day and was raped and left for dead. She was found the next day. From what I hear, she's been pretty messed up ever since.

I thought about Alicia as I entered the cemetery through the huge wrought iron entrance gates. The gates were attached to huge stone pillars, made from stone from the local quarry when this land on the outskirts of town was mostly farm fields and meadows.

I followed a long line of cars and a long line of cars followed me. The road was narrow and uneven, and my car bounced when I hit a pothole. I hated cemeteries more than I hated funerals. I figure when I die, I want to be cremated and my ashes scattered in the ocean. The idea of being stuck in the ground, slowing decaying until there's nothing but bones was morbid to me.

****

Gina

When we passed the stone mausoleum, my throat tightened and my palms got sweaty. I hated this cemetery. My neighbor Alicia was beaten, raped, and left for dead near the mausoleum. That's where the bastard who nearly killed her was hiding. They never found him.

I never told Alicia about Smith. I had considered it, but didn't. Every time I visited Alicia – and I usually tried to see her when I was home visiting mom – she'd make me sit across the room. She never allowed anyone near her. And she never left her house.

Every day, she'd get up and do puzzles. All. Day. Long. Puzzle after puzzle. And it didn't matter what designs they were – landscapes, animals, famous places – she liked them all. But she would never put the same puzzle together twice. The ladies at church held a puzzle drive a couple of times a year to stock Alicia's supply. And I always brought her a few new ones whenever I visited.

I never figured out the whole puzzle thing, though. Why puzzles? It occurred to me that Alicia was like a puzzle with a couple of pieces missing. No matter how hard everyone tried, they couldn't put Alicia completely back together. They couldn't make her whole. There was always a piece or two missing.

Maybe that's why Alicia loved puzzles so much. She could take all the odd shapes and put them together, making something whole and beautiful. It was the one thing in her life that she had control over and could feel good about. The one thing she could figure out.

I was in the car behind the hearse with Sue and Judy. Sue squeezed my hand as we passed the mausoleum. She knew what I was thinking. When we stopped, we waited in the car as the pall bearers removed the coffin from the back of the hearse and carried it over to the burial site sheltered from the sun by a green canvas canopy with scalloped edges.

I jerked when the funeral director opened my door. He took me by the arm and led me to a chair a few feet away from the coffin. My knees buckled as I sat down. Judy and Sue sat on either side of me.

I'm not even sure what the pastor said. Something about walking through the valley of death and fearing no evil; it was all a blur. I couldn't stop looking at the coffin in front of me. Mom was inside that thing. That mahogany thing with the antique hardware and adjustable bed and mattress.

She was going to be put in the ground and I'd never see her again. I knew Dad was down there, and I couldn't help wonder what he looked like. I do this to myself. Think stupid things and then obsess why in the hell I thought them in the first place.

At least the cemetery stone was already on the grave. The only thing I had to arrange was the engraving of Mom's death date. When she had the stone made for Dad, she included her name and birth date. I always thought that was a little morbid, but Mom went on and on about how practical it was. She was right, I know. She was always right. Still, I didn't like seeing her name on the tombstone when I came to visit Dad.

Now, the stone would be finished. Pastor Greg was leading us in a prayer. Sue pulled a few flowers out of the funeral spray on top of the casket and handed them to me. With Judy's help, I stood up, only to be lost in a sea of hands and hugs, people saying they were sorry and that if I needed anything to let them know. I looked out over the crowd that had gathered, and in the back I caught a glimpse of Mike. He caught me looking and nodded. I wondered if he was coming back to the church for the funeral luncheon. After a few more hugs I walked with Sue and Judy to the car. Mike was waiting by the door.

"You go ahead," Sue said. "Judy and I will wait."

****

Mike

I wanted to say something to Gina, but there were so many people that I couldn't get close to her. So I decided to wait by her car. I figured I'd catch her when she went to leave. I wasn't going back to the church for the luncheon, so I wanted her to know that if she needed anything, all she had to do was call.

When she walked up to me, I hugged her and whispered how sorry I was in her ear.

She nodded. "Are you coming back to the church?"

"No. Jack has a baseball game tonight."

"Oh, that's right. You're his coach."

"But, if you need me to come over later..."

Gina shook her head. "No, I'll be fine."

"How long are you staying?" I asked.

"I've got the rest of this week and then I need to head back."

I kicked the loose stones on the road. "Make any decision about the house?"

"Only that I'm going to wait a bit. Let things settle. It's not like I have to do everything before I leave. Sue and Judy will check the house and keep an eye on things until I've made up my mind what I'm going to do."

"Can I see you before you go back?" I asked.

"Yes," Gina said. "I was thinking about tomorrow night. Can you come over for dinner? We can do Chinese takeout or something."

"Jack's at Lisa's tomorrow night so, yeah, that'll work. See you about 7?"

Gina nodded, and I hugged her one more time before turning and walking away.

As I drove out the wrought iron gates I had entered, I noticed for the first time how intricate and beautiful they were. They were forged by hand so many years ago and had stood the test of time.

****

Gina

The funeral luncheon was almost as much of a blur as the funeral. The last thing I wanted to do was eat but the church ladies insisted I go through the buffet line first. And I didn't want them to think I was ungrateful for all they had done.

There was Mrs. Matthews' famous meatballs, Mrs. Nade's macaroni and cheese, and Mrs. Aughenbaugh's cheesy hashbrowns. There were salads of every kind and homemade cakes and pies and cookies. Mom always made baked ziti and I noticed that someone had made it and placed a little note in front of the dish that read: Betty McKenzie's recipe. I scooped out some of the ziti and took a piece of Mrs. Beakler's homemade chocolate cake with peanut butter icing. She always made the best cake, and I hadn't tasted it since dad's funeral.

With Sue and Judy's help, I managed to get through the luncheon. I heard more stories about Mom when she was young and some that were from more recent years. Some of the ladies even brought photos of Mom to share. There was one of Mom and me at one of the church's Mother/Daughter banquets. We wore matching floral dresses mom had made.

By the time I got home, my eyelids felt like lead.

"Are you sure you don't want me to stay?" Sue asked.

"Absolutely. I'm fine. I'm just going to lay down."

"What about later? Dinner or something?"

"I don't think so. Not tonight. I think once I hit that bed I'll be out."

"OK. What about tomorrow night?"

"Mike's coming over."

Sue smiled. "Oh he is, is he? That reminds me, on a scale of one to ten, what was it like? You know, the sex?"

"Twelve," I smiled.

"That good, huh?"

I nodded."That great."

"Oh, Gina. I'm so happy for you. And you're going to talk to him, right?"

"Yes, I'm going to tell him what happened."

"Good. You should have told me. I'm your best friend and you didn't even tell your best friend."

I knew Sue was hurt. I could hear it in her voice. "I couldn't. I really thought he would ruin Mike's life. I know how stupid it sounds now, but back then, at 17, I really believed it."

Sue hugged me. "There were a lot of things we believed back then. I believed that I would meet my prince charming and my life would be a fairy tale. Turned out it was anything but."

"Speaking of prince charming, what about Tom? When are you going out?"

"Well, since I know you'll be with Mike tomorrow night, I'll accept Tom's dinner offer. I was waiting to see what you needed."

I hugged Sue. "Don't worry about me. I'll be fine. Go out with Tom. The guy has adored you forever. You deserve to be adored. And, who knows, maybe they'll be more to this relationship than a few dates."

Sue laughed. "My track record's not very good in that department."

"That's only because you ditch them after a date or two."

"True, but if there was someone I liked, and I do like Tom, it would be more than a date or two."

"Yeah," I said. "Maybe four or five."

We both laughed. It felt good to laugh. I hadn't laughed that hard since the night of the high school reunion when Brad, who thought he was God's gift to women in high school, showed up with a bald head, big ass and a beer gut the size of Mount Everest.

****

Mike

I stopped at the store to buy some wine before picking up the Chinese and heading to Gina's house. When she answered the door, I could tell by her red botchy face that she had been crying.

"I'm starving," she said. "Especially for Moo Goo Gai Pan."

I held up the bag. "Well then, I've got you covered."

I followed Gina into the kitchen. "I got some wine, too. And some beer, just in case."

Gina smiled. "Sounds good."

"So is it wine?" I held up the wine. Or beer?" I held up the beer.

"How about both," Gina laughed.

Gina got some plates from the cabinet. "Do you want to use chop sticks or utensils?"

"Utensils. I can't use those things worth a damn."

I pulled the Moo Goo Gai Pan out of the brown bag along with containers of pork fried rice and chicken and broccoli. "There's a fortune cookie for each of us."

Gina grabbed the cookie out of my hand. I grabbed it back.

"Can't open the fortune cookie until after dinner."

"That's a stupid rule," Gina said.

"You always did want to open your fortune cookie first thing."

"Yeah, and you always made me wait."

I smiled. "Guess some things never change."

I uncorked the bottle of Chardonnay. "Remember the first time we drank wine?"

Gina chuckled. "Yeah, I drank it too fast, got sick and threw up."

"Yeah, on me."

We laughed. I piled my plate with chicken and broccoli and some rice. Gina scooped out some Moo Goo Gai Pan.

"I haven't had Chinese in awhile," I said. "Jack's not big on Chinese."

"Tell me about Jack," Gina asked.

"Jack's great. He's very athletic."

"Doesn't surprise me," said Gina, reaching for her wine glass.

"He does much better in school than I ever did, especially in math. The kid's a whiz."

"Math was never my thing either," Gina said.

"Yeah, I never figured out how you managed to earn an A in calc when the rest of us barely scraped by."

Gina launched into a coughing fit.

"Do you need some water?"

She nodded.

I filled a glass sitting on the counter with water and handed it to her. She took a sip. Her face was red and her eyes were watery.

"You OK?"

"Yeah," she said. "Went down the wrong pipe."

****

Gina

Why did Mike have to bring up the calc class and that stupid A? It totally killed the moment.

"Are you sure you're all right?" Mike asked.

"I'm fine. Just not as hungry as I thought."

"But you said you were starving."

"Yeah, I know. But, well…" I cleared my throat. "Mike, I have something to tell you. It's about that A."

"The calc class A?"

I nodded. "I didn't really earn the A."

"But I saw it on your report card. You showed it to me."

"I didn't say I didn't get an A," I reminded him. "I said that I didn't *earn* it."

Mike shook his head. "I'm confused. Maybe you should start at the beginning."

I sighed. "It's all part of what I started to tell you the other night."

Mike stopped eating and pushed his plate away. "I don't understand. You didn't sleep with Coach Smith to get the A did you?"

"Oh, God, Mike, No. I'd never sleep with that bastard."

Tears exploded from my eyes. "He raped me. I was babysitting and he came home and he was drunk. I tried to leave to go home but he wouldn't let me. He grabbed me and threw me on the floor and gagged me with a tea towel and pulled up my sundress and took off my underwear and…"

Mike bolted out of his chair and pulled me off of mine and wrapped his arms around me. "Damn, Gina. Why didn't you tell me? My God. That fuckin' son of a bitch."

I sobbed as Mike led me to the couch.

"It was awful. He told me that if I told anyone, he'd make sure you'd sit the bench. He wouldn't play you no matter how good you were, no matter what anyone else said. But if I didn't say a word, he'd make sure you played and he'd reach out to college scouts on your behalf. I knew how much you wanted to play baseball at your dad's alma mater, how important it was to you, even more so after your dad's Lou Gehrig's diagnosis, and I just couldn't let him take that dream away from you."

"Jesus fuckin' Christ, Gina. You were my dream. You've always been my dream. Don't you see? You were always more important to me than baseball – than anything."

I grabbed more tissues from the box on the end table. "I was 17 and stupid. I loved you so much and I didn't want you to get hurt. I thought I was doing what was best for you."

Mike ran his fingers through his thick hair. "That fuckin' bastard. And you didn't tell anyone? Not even Sue? All because you were protecting me?"

I nodded. "I had no idea that I would end up hurting you more. I thought that you'd get over me, and go on with your life. And you did. With Lisa."

"But I never felt about Lisa the way I felt about you. Lisa and I were best friends for a long time before it became more. Lisa fell in love with me. I loved her but not in the same way. I thought that being best friends would be enough. But it wasn't. It was wrong. I hurt Lisa and I feel lousy about that. To be honest, I wasn't half the husband the man she's married to is."

****

Mike

The wheels wouldn't stop spinning in my head. "It's all starting to make sense now. The way you pulled away every time I touched you. And here I thought it was me."

"It was never you, Mike. I loved you. I didn't want Smith to hurt you. I just didn't realize how the rape would affect me. And believe me when I say that it has affected my entire life."

"Is that why you do what you do?"

Gina nodded. "Yes, I prosecute bastards like him, make them pay for what they did to innocent victims who can't fight for themselves. And every time I win a case, I not only win for the victim, but also for me."

"But my God, Gina. Did you ever get any help? I mean, that type of thing messes people up."

"Oh, I was messed up. For a long time. I didn't get counseling until after college. I thought I would eventually get over it, but I was wrong. I never did. It was like a virus that I couldn't shake. Some days were better than others, but even on the good days I knew it was there, lurking beneath the surface."

"What about your mom? Did she suspect anything was wrong?"

"She thought my moods were those of a typical teenager. I never told Mom, although she couldn't figure out why taking self-defense classes were so important to me. I blamed it on college and wanting to make sure if anyone tried something I would be prepared. She bought that. Eventually, I was able to work through the trauma, get past the horrible flashbacks.

"I always knew that someday I would tell you the truth. I felt you deserved to know what really happened. Why I really broke up with you. Not because I didn't love you or care about you or want to spend the rest of my life with you, but because I couldn't deal with the rape, and I hurt you because every time you touched me, and I wanted you to touch me, I'd freeze. I'd smell his beer breath and sweat and feel him violating me. And I know that you didn't understand why I pulled away and I couldn't tell you why, so in the end it was just easier to break up and to let you think that I didn't care. You deserved better and I let you go so you could find someone else who could love you the way I wanted to but couldn't."

I threw a fist into a pillow. "But, Jesus, Gina. Your life could have been so much different. My life could have been so much different. We might have been together instead of spending years apart searching for something we've never found with anyone else."

My tears flowed like beer from an open tap. Gina's confession was like a punch in the gut. It knocked the wind out of me. I never saw it coming. And yet everything was beginning to make sense. All the countless nights I laid in bed wondering what the hell happened that summer night so long ago, and now I knew – finally. And if the bastard wasn't dead, I'd kill him.

"I'm sorry," Gina said. "But when you got married and I ran into you in the pizza shop holding Jack, I thought that you were happy, that your life turned out the way you had wanted. I didn't know that you and Lisa were having problems, and I never would have come between the two of you. I honestly wanted you to be happy, and I thought you were."

I handed Gina another tissue. "Does Sue know now?"

"I told her the other night."

"I bet she was steaming," I said.

Gina nodded. "She told me she went to Smith's grave and spit on it the next day. And she was also upset with Tom."

I shook my head. "What's Tom have to do with any of this?"

Gina took a huge breath. "It's not important."

I put my hands on Gina's shoulders to hold her steady and looked her square in the eyes. "Did Tom know?"

Gina exploded in tears again. "But I didn't know that he knew until the night of our reunion. He confronted me in the car before we walked into the ballroom."

I threw another fist into the pillow. "Tom knew and he didn't do anything?"

"It's not Tom's fault. He was jogging past Smith's house that night. He saw me jump into my car and speed away. He said that Smith stumbled down the driveway waving my underwear. Tom stopped and saw that he was drunk and pulled him inside his house. The coach bragged about what he had done and how he had threatened to hurt you if I said anything. Tom was so furious that he punched him in the eye."

"So that's how he got that black eye?" I asked.

"Yeah. Tom never told anyone. He said he wanted to, but when I didn't say anything, he kept quiet. He thought it was up to me to be the one to tell. He was pissed that I never did. He said he thought about telling you, but didn't because he felt it should come from me. He told me the night of the reunion that I should face the past and tell you what really happened."

"You should have told me twenty years ago. It might have saved us both a lot of heartache."

"True. But you wouldn't have Jack. And Jack is the best thing that's ever happened to you. You said so yourself."

I couldn't argue with Gina about that. Jack was the best of me, and I was grateful that I had him.

"So where do we go from here?" I asked.

"Not sure," Gina said. "I feel so mixed up. When I came home for the class reunion, I obviously wasn't expecting all of this to happen, losing Mom, being with you again. But I need to head back to Florida and my job. I have a life to live there. Trials coming up."

"So that's it?" I threw my arm in the air. "You're walking out on me again?"

"That's not fair. It's not like that. But the reality is that I live in another state. I just can't walk away from that life and my responsibilities."

"Why not?"

"You know why not. I'm not 17 anymore. I just can't pick up and leave. It's not that easy, Mike."

"But you could make a decision to live that life here?" I said. "You could start your own practice."

"There are no guarantees in life, Mike. Even if I gave up everything and moved back home, who's to say things would work out between us."

"Well, I thought they worked out pretty well the other night."

"I don't disagree," Gina said. "But it's not that easy. And I need time to figure things out."

"What? Twenty years wasn't enough?"

"That's a low blow and you know it. I need time. But at least now there are no secrets between us. I've been honest with you about everything. I'll never lie to you again."

"So somehow that's supposed to make me feel better. Christ, this is like déjà vu, same fuckin' couch, only twenty years later.

"It's not like that," Gina said.

"Well, excuse me if it feels like it."

"Mike," Gina said. "Please don't make this any harder than it already is. I need time to figure some things out. I'm not saying goodbye this time; I'm saying I'll see you later."

"Fuck later," I said, taking Gina in my arms and kissing her hard. "I'm not giving you up without a fight this time."

I felt Gina's body respond. She twisted her hands in my hair and arched her back as I kissed a path along her jaw line and down her slender neck. "God, you're beautiful."

Gina moaned, and it only made me want her more. I could feel her body shake. "God, Gina baby. You drive me crazy."

She laid back on the couch and she pulled me toward her, unbuttoning my shirt and kissing my chest.

My hands tangled in her hair as she went lower and lower. I couldn't take it anymore. I slid off my jeans as she ripped off her clothes and our bodies hungrily wrapped around each other. I could smell Gina's fragrant hair and taste her sweet skin.

"Let go, baby," I whispered. "Just let go and feel it."

Gina responded and she matched my rhythm as we slowly picked up speed and exploded in each other's arms, our bodies quivering in the aftermath.

The next morning, I woke up before Gina. After we made love on the couch, we ended up in her bed. I slipped out of bed and tiptoed downstairs without waking her. I was still trying to process everything that she had told me the night before. I knew that Gina needed time to figure things out, and I knew that I needed to give her that time. She was right. Her life was in Florida and my life was here. We'd lived in two different worlds and led completely different lives. I was a fool to think we might have a shot at making something work. It wasn't fair of me to think she'd give everything up for me.

I knew I had to let her go even if it meant my heart would be broken – again. Tears filled my eyes. I found a piece of paper and a pen in the kitchen and left a note.

Sometimes, Gina, the thing we want most is the thing we can't have. This time, I'm the one letting go. I hope you find what you're searching for.
Always, Mike

Chapter 15

Gina

Going back to work was a blessing in a lot of ways. It kept my mind off things, at least during the day. But late at night, when I was alone in my bed in a city that felt cold, I thought about Mike. He was like a favorite song that I couldn't stop singing, a song that gets stuck in your head – and forever in your heart.

Images of us making love played over and over in my mind. I hadn't been that turned on or felt that connected to any guy in twenty years. Just thinking about Mike taking me so high took my breath away. It was sad to think I might not ever feel that way again. Deep down, I wanted Mike. But he had a life that I wasn't a part of, a young son that he was helping to raise. He needed to be there and I needed to be here. Nothing would change that.

I pulled out the note he left on the kitchen table.

Sometimes, Gina, the thing we want most is the thing we can't have. This time, I'm the one letting go. I hope you find what you're searching for.
Always, Mike

I hoped that I found what I was searching for, too.

****

I started running again, but lately I've been so tired that I don't even have the energy to do that. I ran into Rob and Molly at the park and we sat on a bench and talked for a long time. The tingle I felt the first time I ran into Rob, wasn't as strong, and I knew why. I was thinking about Mike. When Rob asked me out, I had to be honest. I told him I ran into my old boyfriend at my high school reunion and had to sort out my feelings.

"I see," he said, brushing Molly's coat. "That's usually the way it goes for me. Boy meets girl. Boy likes girl. Girl meets better boy." He laughed.

I turned toward him so that I was looking straight into his eyes. "I just don't think it's fair for me to start something with you when I have so much to figure out."

Rob nodded. "Thanks for being honest, Gina. I like you, but I definitely don't want to get mixed up in something until your head is on straight."

He stood up. "You have my number. So call me if things ever change."

I nodded. "Thanks, Rob. I will."

He scratched the top of Molly's head. "Ready, girl? Let's go home."

I waved and smiled. Home. That word I couldn't get out of my mind. Where was home for me? Here didn't seem like home as much as it once did. When I was home, that seemed like home, even after Mom died. But if that was home, what was I doing here?

When I got back to my condo, there was a message from Sue. I grabbed a drink and called.

"How are things going with Tom?" I asked.

"Unbelievable," Sue said. "I've never been this happy. We see each other every night."

I could hear the happiness in Sue's voice. It was higher than Chloe's piccolo, and the words seemed to dance on her tongue. "Does Chloe like him?"

"I think she's more in love with him than I am."

"Whoa! Sues. Did you just say the L word?"

There was a pregnant pause. "Well, I might have said the L word."

I shrieked and started to dance around my living room with the phone sandwiched between my ear and my shoulder. "Does he know? Did you tell him?" I wish I was with Sue because I know she would be dancing, too.

"Oh, God, no. Not yet." Sue said.

"What are you waiting for?"

"Well, the last time it didn't work out so well for me."

I stopped dancing and sat down on my couch, tucking my legs beside me. "But this isn't like last time. You've known Tom all of your life. He's been in love with you since high school. He would never do anything to hurt you."

"I know," Sue said. "It's just a scary step."

"I get that. I really do. But sometimes you've got to go for home. If you never get off third base, there's no chance of ever getting to home plate."

"You're a fine one to talk."

"What's that mean?"

"I'm talking about Mike. You've been in love with him your entire life, and just when he's back in your life, you let him go."

"He's the one who walked away."

"Only because he thought that's what you wanted. And, besides, you could have gone after him."

"But what about my life here? Sues? I have a job. An important job. I just can't walk away from my responsibilities."

"Your work has always been your life, Gina. But maybe it's time that there's more to it, and Mike might be that more. Plus, lawyers can find work anywhere."

I bit my lip. I knew there was a lot of truth in what she was saying. I hated that about Sue. She had a way of cutting through the crap and saying what I needed but didn't want to hear.

"Chloe and I ran into him and Jack today at Pizza Palace," Sue said.

"Did he ask about me?"

"Of course he asked about you. He wanted to know if the house sold yet. What we were doing with the contents."

I choked on my sip of water. "The contents?"

"Yeah. I told him that you had put what you wanted to keep in storage and had arranged for an auction house to clean out the rest."

"Anything else?"

"My, aren't we the nosey one." Sue laughed. "He asked what auction house and when you were coming home again."

"That's strange."

"What?"

"The auction house. That he asked about that," I said.

"I thought it was a little odd, too, but whatever. So what's the update on the last showing? Have you heard from your real estate agent?"

"I heard from her earlier. She said the couple seemed interested but wanted to look around some more. I think they were concerned about the age of the furnace and roof. I don't blame them. Whoever buys the house will have to replace both within a couple of years."

I could hear Chloe in the background telling Sue to tell me something.

"What's Chole want?"

"She wants me to tell you that she made the distinguished honor roll."

"Awesome," I said. "I know she must feel great about that, especially since she worked so hard to bring up that math grade."

"Yeah, speaking about feeling great, are you still so tired?"

"Yeah. I think that it's because I'm depressed. When I'm depressed, all I want to do is sleep."

"When I'm depressed, all I want to do is eat," Sue said.

"Well, I go to the doctors tomorrow for a checkup. He sent me for blood work a few days ago so maybe that'll show something."

"Yeah, you could be anemic," Sue said. "I had that problem before. But you ought to ask her about getting something for the depression. Mom was on something for a while after Dad died. Just took the edge off. Helped her cope a little better."

I stretched out on the sofa, leaning my head against the armrest. "I thought about that. We'll see."

"Are you still going through with the insemination?" Sue asked.

"Yes. I'm not getting any younger and I want a baby. Losing Mom has made me even more determined to make this happen. I've waited long enough."

****

227

Mike

I wasn't expecting to run into Sue and Chloe at Pizza Palace. I couldn't help asking about Gina. She was all I had thought about lately. It was more than the incredible sex we had, although I had to admit that I missed that. It was the way she made me feel. I wanted to call her, but I didn't want to pressure her. When I slipped out of bed and left her that note, I put the ball in her court. Damn how I hoped she'd pick up the ball and run in my direction. I looked for her every day, but she never came.

"You not hungry, Dad?" Jack asked.

"Not too much."

He pointed to the half-eaten slice of pepperoni pizza on my plate. "I'll finish that if you're not going to."

I smiled. Jack was growing as fast as my grass. I pushed the plate toward him. "Go right ahead."

"Dad, did you always want to be an engineer?"

"No," I told him. "I wanted to be a professional baseball player."

"Like me," Jack smiled.

"Yep, just like you. Only I wasn't as good as you. Keep working hard and who knows."

Jack smiled and took the last bite. "What's for dessert?"

"You're still hungry after eating all that?"

Jack nodded.

"There's some ice cream in the freezer. Oh, and I got a bottle of chocolate syrup at the store."

Jack got up to get the ice cream and I cleared the table.

"How's your little sister these days?" I asked.

"She's teething. Mom rubs something on her gums but it doesn't help much. And she's all slobbery. Kind of gross."

I laughed. I was glad Jack had a sibling, though. I remember how much Gina hated being an only child. She was the only one in our group who didn't have any brothers or sisters. Guess when Gina has her baby, she'll be an only child, too. I wondered if she would name her baby Daisy. She's loved that family name forever.

****

Gina

"How long have you been feeling like this?" Dr. McGuire asked.

"A few weeks. But with my mom dying, I've had so much to take care of. And when I'm depressed, all I want to do is sleep."

Dr. McGuire opened my chart on her laptop. "Let's take a look at your blood work."

She studied the screen and a smile slid onto her face. "Have you seen the fertility specialist?"

I nodded. "Yes. We've talked and have plans."

229

"Well, congratulations. It looks like the insemination has worked."

I was so startled that I jumped and almost fell off the examination table. "But I. I didn't have the insemination. Because of my mom dying, we had to reschedule." My leg started shaking and I could feel my face heating up.

Dr. McGuire pursed her thin lips. "Well, then. Maybe you got some explaining to do to someone."

"Are you serious? I'm pregnant? That's why I've been so tired?" My hands clutched the sides of my head.

Dr. McGuire smiled. "Yes, you're pregnant. And apparently you got pregnant the old-fashion way."

"Oh. My. God. I, I…"

"Everything OK, Gina?" Dr. McGuire asked. "This is what you wanted, right?"

I sighed a million years. "Yes. Absolutely. I just didn't think. You're right. I have some explaining to do. Don't get me wrong, I've never been happier. I just didn't expect it."

I could tell by the way Dr. McGuire scrunched her nose that she was confused.

"I'm sorry, you're probably wondering what the hell is going on in my life that I didn't expect it," I said. "And I don't want you to think I'm a slut who sleeps around."

"Gina, I…"

"It's OK. I want you to know. I reconnected with my high school boyfriend at our 20th class reunion.

He was the love of my life – still is. One thing led to another and, well, now I'm pregnant. I'm not complaining; it's just that the thought never crossed my mind. I had planned to get pregnant from insemination, not from Mike. But there's no man's baby I'd rather be carrying. But it does mean I have some explaining to do."

****

Mike

When I came home and found Gina sitting on my front porch steps, my knees buckled. She looked so hot in her jeans and white button-down shirt. I noticed immediately that she was wearing the silver heart necklace I had given her when we were in high school. It was the necklace she wore in her formal graduation photo, the one hanging on her Mom's wall.

She stood up and I hugged her.

"Nice necklace," I said.

Gina touched the necklace with her hand. "I wasn't sure you'd notice."

"And I wasn't sure I'd see you again," I said, motioning her to follow me into the house.

She saw the plaid couch right away, sitting against the wall. "So that's why you wanted to know about the auction house?"

I smiled. "How'd you…"

"Sue told me."

"Of course."

"Why did you want that ratty old thing anyway?"

"Good memories, I guess."

"They weren't all good?"

"True. But most of them were. Want something to drink?"

Gina shook her head no.

I pointed to the plaid couch. "For old time's sake?"

We sat down on the couch, me at the far end and Gina right next to me. We turned toward one another.

"So are you just back to take care of house stuff?" I asked.

"Sort of."

Gina bit her bottom lip. "Remember I told you that there would be no more secrets between us."

I nodded and took a deep breath. I could tell by the way Gina was wringing her hands that she had something pretty important to say.

Gina looked down toward her lap. "I. I. She sighed. "This is going to be harder than I thought."

I lifted Gina's chin and brushed the hair back off her face. "Gina, it's OK. Whatever you have to tell me, it's OK. I'll understand."

Tears gathered in Gina's eyes and her smile tiptoed back onto her face. "Well, I'm pregnant."

I'm not sure what I was expecting, but I wasn't expecting that. I knew that Gina had wanted a baby and had seen a fertility specialist. But I guess I thought that with everything that happened, she might wait awhile. I know she had planned on having her mom's help. Now she would be all on her own. Still, if that's what she wanted, I was happy for her.

I ran my fingers through my hair. "So the fertility thing worked, huh? I think it's great that you're pregnant. I know how much you wanted a child."

Gina bit her bottom lip. "Uh, I didn't get pregnant that way."

My heart felt like it was being squeezed. I couldn't believe what I was hearing. All I could think about since Gina left was being with her. I couldn't imagine not making love to her again. It was incredible sex. The way our bodies fit – perfectly. She was everything I ever wanted and just when I thought we might have a chance, she tells me there's another guy. "Oh, I see. Do you love him?"

"Very much," she said. "I've always loved him."

I thought I was going to die. It was happening again. My heart was being broken on this damn plaid couch – again. Why the fuck did I buy the old ratty thing anyway?

"I don't know what to say, Gina. I'm not going to lie. You're all I thought about since you left. I was hoping that if I gave you time and didn't pressure you that you'd figure things out. Maybe even come back. And then, when I saw you sitting on the porch steps, and the necklace, I thought maybe you had."

"I did."

"Did what?" I asked.

"Come back."

"Jesus Christ," I said. "The guy lives in the area?"

Gina nodded.

I got up from the couch. "God damn, Gina. I can't believe this is happening again. My lousy luck."

"Mike, I've only been with one guy in the last two years."

"One? But what about?"

Gina smiled.

"Oh my God, Gina," I said, taking her in my arms. "Oh my God, baby. I can't believe it. Why didn't you just come out and tell me?"

"I was trying to. I thought when I told you that I always loved the guy that you'd get it."

I kissed Gina long and hard and when we were done we left a trail of clothes to my bedroom.

****

Gina

Lying in Mike's arms felt so right. Like it was where I belonged. I knew we had a lot to figure out, but I also knew that I had found my way home. That was a happy ending to our book.

I drew circles on his chest with the tips of my fingers. Mike kissed the top of my head.

"So did you sell your mom's house?" Mike asked.

"I had a couple who were interested in it and they gave me an offer. But I ended up taking it off the market."

Mike sat up and looked down at me. "Why?"

I smiled. "I figured the house is twice the size of yours and if we're going to make a go of it, we'd need a bigger house – enough bedrooms for us and Jack and the baby."

Mike leaned down and kissed me again and his lips trailed down my neck and chest and before I knew it we were making love once again.

Mike and I bounced down the stairs like a couple of kids. I was starving and we decided to go out for Chinese.

"There's something I want to show you before we grab a bite to eat." Mike said.

He pulled me by my hand to the brown, plaid couch.

"The reason I wanted this sofa is because of what it contains."

I scratched my head. "The stuffing?"

Mike laughed. "Twenty years ago, on the night you broke up with me, I was going to give you something. I wanted to surprise you. I unzipped the cushion and stuck it in there for safe keeping."

"Which cushion?"

"The right one. It's still there. I checked."

I walked over to the cushion and unzipped the back of it. There was a blue, plastic ring and two slips of paper inside a sandwich baggie. I opened the bag and took out the first note.

Gina, I love you more than anything. This ring is my promise that you're the only girl I will ever love. I want to grow old with you and have kids with you. I hope you accept this ring as a token of my love. When I can afford it, I'll get you a big diamond.
Love, Mike

The tears came hard and heavy, "Oh Mike. This has been in that cushion all this time?"

Mike nodded. "When I saw your mom still had the couch, I checked to see if it was there when you were out of the room. I felt the plastic bag right away."

I picked up the other slip of paper. "You wrote two notes?"

Mike scratched his head. "No, just one."

I opened the other note. I recognized the floral stationery immediately. I had bought it for Mom one Christmas. "It's from Mom."

Mike's jaw dropped. I read the note.

Gina, if you find this note, it's because you were meant to. Always follow your heart, and you will never go wrong.
Love you bunches and bunches, Mom

"She must have found the bag and added the note," Mike said.

"And she never said anything," I added. "So like her."

I took the ring out of the bag and Mike slipped it on my finger.

"Came out of the bubblegum machine in front of the grocery store," Mike said. "It cost a quarter, but it was worth a lot more."

Mike got down on one knee, "Gina, I want you in my life. I've never stopped loving you. I want to marry you, raise our child together, if you'll have me. Gina, will you marry me?"

My mouth quivered and I could taste the runaway tears. Everything I had ever wanted was coming true and for the first time in a long time, I felt like I had found my way home. Like Mom said, I listened to my heart and it was telling me to stay.

"I thought you'd never ask," I said. I leaned in to kiss him and the minute our lips touched I giggled.

Mike pulled back to look me in the eyes. "What are you laughing about?"

"Just remembering what I wrote in your yearbook. Do you remember?"

Mike cleared his throat. "Remember, you said you'd love me even when I'm old and wrinkled and have white hair and false teeth."

A firework smile burst onto my face. "And do you still feel that way?"

"I'll show you," said Mike, wrapping his arms around me and chasing me with urgent kisses. "Oh, Gina, baby. You drive me crazy."

He pulled away and I pulled him back.

"But what about the Chinese food?" he asked.

My lips trailed down his chest. "The moo moo gai pan can wait."

Gina's Classmates

Julie (Yearbook post)

Gina,

To a cool girl who always seems to be there just in case someone needs her. You are a very super person. You have never made me feel dumb and you never seem to mind that I'm not exactly a "scholar" – you talk and laugh and are friends with me anyway. We'll have to do something together sometime. I wish you much happiness and lots of luck in whatever you do. You have a lot going for you – you are just a swell person!!! I hope we never lose touch! Have a nice summer!!

Always, Julie

....

The thing I remember about Julie is her skin. She had the most beautiful skin, especially to a teenager who battled acne with a cabinet full of crap that left my skin dry and red and flaky – not smooth like hers. She had an easy smile, like a morning glory's petals unfurling when they are kissed by a new day.

We first met in junior high social studies class. Even then she was a beauty. And it's her beauty that attracted the guys, although they never seemed to hang around for long.

One time in high school, I found her crying in the bathroom. Her mascara ran down her pink cheeks and her hair was a tangled mess of black.

"Julie, what's wrong?" I asked.

"Everything," she said. "My life sucks. I'm tired of being used."

I put my arm around her and she fell into my shoulder. "Then stop."

She pulled back and looked at me with swollen raccoon eyes. "You just don't get it. I'm not like you. Smart and all."

"Don't say that," I said. "You just have to work a little harder. And I can help."

The next day, I saw her with a new guy. She never called me for homework help, and we never did anything together outside of school. She ran with a different crowd that I never wanted to be a part of. The last time I saw her was at graduation. She had gone through probably a dozen guys our senior year.

I was in college when Mom called to tell me Julie was found dead in her bedroom. According to one of Mom's golf buddies who knew the family, it was an overdose. There was no note, nothing.

Sometimes, I look back on that bathroom conversation and I wish I would have done more. Truth is it probably wouldn't have made a difference. Julie was lost long before I found her. I never understood how so much beauty could be so ugly, how a life ends before it ever really begins.

James Robert (Yearbook post)

Gina,

Oh well, here I go again trying to think of what to write in someone's yearbook. It just so happens that yours is the hardest. You've affected my life so many times and in so many ways that I don't know what to say. You made me realize things about other people and about myself. I've done super stupid things that I wish I could do over, but once you do them it's too bad. Knowing what you would do in the situation really helps me a lot because believe it or not, I know you better than I know myself. I just don't have any confidence (sometimes) and I always expect the worst (but that's good in some cases, because I'm ready for the worst when it does happen). As I was saying you know what you want and you stick to it, because you have a great head on your shoulders (wise and sharp looking).

The time I've spent with you over the past year has really been great. I know I'm probably a pain in your ass, but I've been doing a lot of thinking lately and aside from one incident, I've changed a lot. I hope you don't change because you don't have to (you shouldn't). I'm starting to run out of space and I have a hundred other things to write, so I'll sum it up and say: "You're one hell of a friend and I hope you keep in touch with me even when you're in your 60s." You're closer to me than any one of my other friends so keep out of trouble and don't get that pretty little head of yours into a bum situation.

Love always,

J.R.

....

Every time I'm home visiting my mom, I drive by the house where J.R. grew up. I loved J.R. like a brother and felt badly that I wasn't able to love him in the way he loved me. I tried to, but it just didn't work. Maybe I was afraid of ruining what we had. I was closer to him than I was to many of my girlfriends, and there were things that we talked about that I could never have talked about with them.

I remember our last long talk. It was the week before we both started our freshman year in college. We jumped on his cycle and went to his favorite talking spot, miles outside of town. We lay side by side on the spongy hillside, staring up at the black sky. J.R. loved coming to this spot, especially on a clear night because the stars were so bright. He always pointed out the constellations and then shared the stories behind them. It was J.R. who explained to me that the Big Dipper and Little Dipper weren't constellations but asterisms. I was always amazed at how much he knew about totally random stuff.

That was the night that he told me that he was glad he was going away to college. That he needed to get away from me. That he just couldn't take loving me as much as he did and seeing me with another guy. He didn't blame me. He said it wasn't my fault that he fell in love with someone who didn't return his feelings. But that he needed a chance to see if he could love someone as much as he loved me.

I know I shouldn't have, but I kissed him that night. The way a girlfriend kisses a boyfriend. I needed to see how it felt, to see if maybe I was wrong. So I leaned over him and bent down to find his lips and he rolled on top of me and kissed me with so much passion I could hardly breathe. But then he stopped. Suddenly. And sat up.

"I don't want you like this," he said. "Don't give me what you think I want. But if you ever want me, really, really want me, you know where I'll be."

When he dropped me off that night, we hugged.

"Sorry if I screwed things up," I said.

"You didn't screw things up. It's just that I can't handle feeling the way I do about you. I've tried so hard for the past year and I just think I need a break. It's not you. It's me. I need to get my head on straight. Quit wishing for something that's never going to happen."

It was the last time I saw J.R. It was like he went away to college and vanished. I tried finding him from time to time, but I didn't have any luck. I always wondered if he had found someone who loved him as much as he loved me. I hoped that he found someone who loved him more.

Brad (Yearbook post)

Gina,

To one of the nicest looking girls I know. Keep up the good looks and if you're ever free, let me know.

Brad

....

Dick! That's what Brad was. I guess I should feel honored that he referred to me as nice looking. Even if someone had offered me a hundred bucks to go out with him, I wouldn't have. The guy was a jerk with a capital J.

He thought that his GQ-ish looks entitled him to whatever girl he wanted. And, of course, most girls oohed and aahed over his defined pecs and bulging biceps. And his tight ass. Not me. I wasn't the least bit interested, which pissed him off, I think.

He was one of the guys who used Julie and when he got tired of her, discarded her like a sweaty workout towel.

I hope he's fat and out of shape. And ugly. Serves him right. He broke so many hearts and never once said sorry. Screw you, Brad. (That felt good.)

Karen (Yearbook post)

Gina,

You're a real crazy girl but an awful lot of fun to be around. You can brighten anybody's life with your smiling face. I wish you the best of luck in all your future attempts.

Love, Karen

....

Karen got pregnant our senior year and had her daughter the summer after we graduated. She married the guy, who was older, but it didn't last long. Maybe a year.

Karen was a good athlete. No matter what sport she tried she was good at it. Basketball. Softball. Tennis. You name it and she could play it – and play it well. I always thought she'd go to college to become a gym teacher. She did go to college, eventually. She worked during the day and went to school at night. She and her daughter, Sarah, lived with her parents, who helped out a lot.

It took Karen many years, but she finally earned a business degree. I guess after that she kept on going because Mom sent me a newspaper clipping announcing that she had earned her MBA.

One Christmas break, Mom and I ran into Karen at the mall. She was obviously pregnant. She introduced me to her significant other, a beautiful woman with long, silky black hair and an hour-glass figure I would die for. I must have looked surprised because Karen leaned over and whispered. "Yeah, I know, it surprises everyone. Isn't she gorgeous?" And then she looked at Mia and smiled.

Karen patted her stomach. "And, as you can see, we're having a baby."

Without me asking, Karen explained that she and Mia wanted to have a child together. Karen said that since she loved being pregnant, they decided she would carry the child. But the egg was Mia's, fertilized with donor sperm.

"So this one should look like Mia," said Karen, casting Mia another look.

"Do you know what you're having?" Mom asked.

"A boy," Karen said. "We wanted a boy since we already have a daughter."

It was definitely more information than Mom or I needed to know, but it made me smile. I had forgotten how open Karen was.

I learned that Karen met Mia while studying for her MBA and that they had been together ever since. Mia seemed nice and Karen seemed happier than I ever remember her being.

Tom (Yearbook post)

Gina,

To a real nice girl I got to know in chem and calc class. Never forget all the bad luck you had with test tubes during unknowns. Good luck with all you do in life and with that special someone.

AFA, Tom

....

I hated unknowns in chemistry. The teacher would give us a substance and we'd have to run tests to determine what it was. It was a real pain in the ass. The worse thing about chem, though, was the goggles we had to wear. Talk about feeling like a complete dork. The goggles always left marks on my face, which seemed to last for hours afterward. And they messed up my makeup, which when you're seventeen and vain is a really big deal.

Tom, on the other hand, loved chemistry. Sometimes, when the teacher wasn't looking, he'd swap test tubes with me, figure out my unknown, and give it back to me. He always had my back in chem.

He went to college to be a pharmacist and works in my hometown. Mom sees him when she picks up her cholesterol medicine at the drug store, and she said he always asks about me. He's not married, but Mom says she sees him walking his golden retriever in the park by the elementary school where she walks with her best friend, Judy.

Bob (Yearbook post)

Gina,

To a nice girl with a great personality. Never forget our wild homeroom. Good luck always.

Bob

....

Bob came to school high every morning. He reeked of weed. I asked him once why he got high before school. He said it made him feel better.

Bob was my friend. We never did anything together and he wasn't in any of my classes, but he was the type of guy who would be the first to help you if you had a problem. He wasn't book smart, but he was street smart. And he was good with cars. One look at the grease embedded in his nails and the black stains on his fingers told you he spent most of his time under the hood of a car.

I ran into Bob a few years after school at the grocery store. He didn't smell like weed and he had a little boy with him.

"This is Luke," he said. "He's three."

So Bob became a dad. He told me he had his own garage. He didn't care for the business part of things, but his girlfriend took care of that. He seemed happy, and I was happy for him.

I remember some of my friends asking me why I talked to a pothead. To them, Bob was from the other side of the tracks, not good enough to associate with. But I liked Bob. And, to be honest, I think that if I had ever gotten into trouble or needed help, Bob would have helped me quicker than many of them would have.

It's true what they say about not judging a book by its cover. Sometimes the cover is tattered or maybe it's missing altogether. That doesn't mean what you find inside isn't worth your time. What a shame that people couldn't look beyond the cover to discover the Bob I had. I wonder now if they realize how foolish they had been. Maybe it would have made a difference in his life. I know it would have in theirs.

Ray (Yearbook post)

Gina,

To a nice girl I got to know better in the last year. Good luck at all your future attempts.

Ray

....

Ray didn't have many friends. He was a little backward. When you spoke to him face to face, he would never look you in the eyes. He always looked at the floor. That absolutely drove me insane. I hate when people don't look at me when I talk to them. But I understood that Ray was a little different so I tried to cut him some slack.

249

Ray was a gifted artist. I sat beside him in history class and he spent the entire period drawing. Mostly, he drew comic strips but he also sketched stuff he saw in class – like the wilting geranium in the clay pot sitting on the windowsill.

I tried to peek once to get a better view, but he covered his work with his arm. He didn't like sharing his drawings. Probably didn't want people to make fun of his work. That's why he was mortified one day when The Palmer-nator (aka Mrs. Palmer) caught him drawing in class.

The Palmer-nator walked back to Ray's desk before he had a chance to stash his work. She grabbed it and held it up for everyone to see. It was a sketch of her. Ray slid as far down in his seat as he could. It was the last time he drew in her class. I always thought that Ray drew because it was his way of expressing himself. I wonder if he still draws.

Diane (Yearbook post)

Gina,

To a funny, hilarious, and extremely rib-killing person. No matter where you are you bring a smile to everyone's face. You also bring tears to their eyes!! I'll never forget the time you told us about having to fart during your violin recital!

Diane

....

So for the rest of my life Diane is going to remember me as the-girl-who-had-to-fart-during-her-violin-recital. Yeah, well, it did happen. I tried to cover it up by playing louder, but it didn't matter. It was one of the most embarrassing moments of my junior high life. Here I was playing the theme from Romeo and Juliet, a piece that I had practiced for months, and farted right in the middle of it. Thank gawd no one said a word. In fact, they acted like they never heard it, which I'm sure they did.

Diane played the tuba, and if you ever saw her 4-foot, 7-inch self carrying that brass beast you'd laugh. Picture Toto hauling the Tin Man. I remember how her parents tried to talk her into playing another instrument, something smaller, like a flute or clarinet, but she refused. Good thing, too, because the tuba took her far.

She got a music scholarship and after earning her teaching degree replaced the band director at our high school. I heard Mr. Mummert was going to retire earlier but really wanted Diane to get the job and waited until she graduated to give her a chance. She did her student teaching under him and was really excited about teaching in the school that she graduated from.

Diane married a trumpet player. One of my good friends, Cookie, who attended their wedding, told me it was music themed. A small tuba and trumpet topped the cake. Each table was named after a favorite song. The place cards looked like concert tickets with the guests' names on them and sheet music was scattered on the tables. Each guest also received a music notes keychain.

I quit the violin when I got to high school. There were so many other things I wanted to try. I still have it, though. Every once in awhile, I get it out. The A string is missing and the bow needs to be re-haired. My cake of rosin is worn down the middle from years of rubbing it up and down my bow.

I wish I would have stuck with it. Why is it that when we give up something it's so hard to get it back?

Peter (Yearbook post)

Gina,

To a really nice girl I met in homeroom. Take care.

Peter

....

I'm just going to say it. Peter creeped me out. It seemed like he was always watching me. I'd catch him staring at me in homeroom or in the hallway. His locker was down from mine.

When he asked to sign my yearbook, I didn't want to be a snob and say no. But I was glad he didn't write much.

No one has ever made me feel so uncomfortable. I was never afraid of Peter. It's not like I thought he would hurt me. His stares were more of a longing – like he wanted to be with me in a way I would never want to be with him. Infatuation, I guess. A secret admirer, only he wasn't as secret as he thought.

I told Mike about the staring once, and he wanted to set Peter straight. I told him to let it go. It wasn't that big of a deal. But I think he had a talk with Peter anyway because the last month of our senior year, I didn't catch Peter staring quite so much.

Cookie (Yearbook post)

Gina,

You're a crazy, crazy girl and we shared so many laughs together this year. I'll miss ya next year. Thanks for always sharing your orange gum and never forget all of the wild times at Jeremy's house! I'm sure you'll be a success and I'll try to keep in touch.

Love, Cookie

....

Funny that Amy – we called her Cookie – thought I was crazy. She was the crazy one. What I liked most about her is that she blazed her own path. Some days, she'd come to school dressed in the wackiest stuff, liked multicolored striped socks with a hounds tooth skirt and stripped shirt. It would look totally ridiculous on me, but on Cookie, it looked perfect.

I admired her for her spirit, and I always wished I could be more like her. Cookie never worried about what others thought of her. She was comfortable in her skin. And confident. Some of my girlfriends made fun of Cookie. But I think deep inside they wished they could be more like her.

It didn't surprise me when Mom sent me a newspaper clipping about a local school district banning some books for sexually explicit content and offensive language and violence. Leading the opposition to the ban was Cookie.

"Where does the censorship end?" she was quoted as saying in the newspaper article.

That was Cookie. Always standing up for what she believed in, even if was the unpopular thing to do.

Mom asked me how Amy got the nickname Cookie. It started in first grade. She always brought her lunch and every day it included Oreo cookies. So we started to call her Cookie.

Some days, if she wasn't really hungry, she'd auction off her cookies. I learned to always have a nickel or two in my pocket just in case.

Cookie's the one who taught me how to eat Oreos to get the most out of them. She'd pull the cookie apart, scrap the crème off with her two front teeth and then eat the chocolate wafers. I asked her once why she didn't lick off the icing. She said it made her tongue tired, especially if they were double-stuffed.

Robby, who always sat with us at lunch, ate his cookie whole. He liked to taste everything together. She told him she thought that was lame. That eating Oreos wasn't something to be rushed, but enjoyed.

Funny the things you remember. I hadn't thought about our Oreo eating in decades.

Margaret (Yearbook post)

Gina,

To one of my dearest friends that I love very much. Always think of me as a friend and remember that I'm here if you need me. Never forget all the good times we had. Good luck in everything you do, and take care of Mike. When I look at you, I realize that you are aggressive and you'll go far. Remember me always.

Luv ya, Maggie

....

I never thought of myself as aggressive, but I guess I am. I wonder if that's a bad thing. Maybe yes and maybe no. Guess it depends on the situation. I think it's worked well for me most of my life, but there was at least one time when being too aggressive cost me a friend.

Maggie was more of a follower than a leader. She was content to stand in the stage wings and let others bask in the spotlight. I used to get so mad at her for letting others take credit for her ideas. I told her it was like working your ass off to lose 20 pounds and then continuing to wear huge shirts – no one will notice the results of all your hard work. She always said that it didn't matter. That she knew and that was good enough.

Today, Maggie is definitely not in anyone's shadows. Although every chance she gets, she steps aside and lets those who work for her bathe in the glory. After finishing college, she started working in the textile industry and climbed to the top, eventually becoming general manager and vice president of Dye Works Inc. She chairs the board of directors of the local hospital and Mom has sent me newspaper clippings over the years about her receiving awards for her charitable work.

Knowing Maggie, I'm sure she is embarrassed by the accolades.

Ellen (Yearbook post)

Gina,

To a great friend. You're always there to help and listen to me whenever I'm down. You've brought me back to earth many times, and I'm very grateful for that. So if there is ever a time when you need help, don't forget that I'm here. Next year you'll be going off to college. Our gang will be spread apart. I hope we keep in touch by writing to each other and visiting.

I'm looking forward to spending a weekend at college with you. There are so many things that we all have to experience yet. I hope that you and Mike will keep that great relationship you two have. I think you have finally found a love that is good and true and I can see what he does for you.

Never forget all of the fun times that we shared these past four years. I hope there are many more to come. Good luck with everything you do and keep in touch over the summer. I'll see you at the prom.

Love, El

....

Ellen was right about one thing, after high school we all went in different directions. We kept in touch the first year, but then we started to drift apart.

The things that bound us together in high school no longer existed. We didn't cheer together. We weren't class officers. We weren't in the senior class play or planning social events for the student body. We were no longer the big fishes in a little pond but little fishes in very big ponds – and the ponds were worlds apart.

I had thought our friendship meant more, and I'm mad that I didn't do more to keep it intact.

Guess you always think there's time to catch up and make things right, and then time runs out.

After high school, Ellen went to culinary school. I wonder if she's cooking at some Five-star restaurant like she dreamed she would.

Becky (Yearbook post)

Gina,

Well, I believe you know what I have to say. I have so much to tell you but I'm not a very good writer. But I'll try my best. Sorry for being such a bitch this year but I had problems. Thank you for standing by me and for understanding. I sure do hope that you get everything out of life because you deserve it. But I don't have to worry about that because I know you will go after what you want and not stop for anything. If you ever need me to support you or back you up for anything, you know I will be there.

Love, Becky

....

Becky was a bitch our senior year. But only the second half. It started after Christmas break. I think something happened when she went to visit her older brother in Chicago. She left the day after Christmas and spent the week with him, including New Year's Eve. I tried talking to her about it every now and then, but that just made her bitchier.

Finally, a week or two before graduation, she seemed to come around. Whatever she was pissed about, whatever happened I guess she made peace with it. I was glad to have the old Becky back. As much as I always tried to support her, even I was getting tired of her whiny, bitchy self.

Becky went into the Air Force right after high school, and I'm sad to say we lost touch. Mom sent me a newspaper clipping when she finished basic training. There was a photo of Becky. I remember the photo because she wasn't smiling, and Becky always had the most beautiful smile.

Lynn (Yearbook post)

Gina,

To a really terrific girl that I've known practically all of my life. Remember all the fun in student council and all of Mr. Flannigan's "speeches." Of course, don't forget all the work we put into making the prom a hit. I'm glad we have stayed friends all of these years, and I hope that we will always be friends. If you ever need me to plan anything for you, let me know.

Love, Lynn

....

Lynn was always a great planner. Very organized and detail oriented. She made a great class president, an office we had to beg her to go for because no one else in our group wanted all of the responsibilities. And, to be honest, none of us was as good as Lynn at planning and making sure things got done.

It didn't surprise me that she became an events planner for a swanky country club. I always thought that if I needed a wedding planner, I'd want Lynn.

When we planned the prom, she kept everyone on task and focused. She thought of details that the rest of us hadn't given any thought to – like the order of the people in the receiving line. That's how she was; she left nothing to chance. Every decision was backed up with sound reasoning and she always had a Plan B. Her obsessing drove me a little crazy at times, but she made everything she was a part of better.

Joe (Yearbook post)

Gina,

To the one girl who I think has the best personality out of anybody I know. Always keep those good looks and special smile. I wish you luck at anything you try to accomplish in the future. You are very special to me as a friend.

Take care, Joe

....

I've never seen anyone battle drugs like Joe. He started drinking heavily our junior year in high school and then got into pot and other stuff. I liked Joe. I always tried to talk to him about what was going on. I knew he was in trouble. He always said that he could handle it and that he could quit anytime he wanted. We both knew that wasn't true.

I watched as his smiling eyes turned into a blank stare. As he lost weight and stopped caring about his appearance. As he started skipping school and his grades plummeted. Looking back, I'm surprised he graduated.

Watching Joe was like watching a fly become ensnared in a spider's web. I wanted to rescue him, but I didn't know how.

He called me one night when I was in college. He was crying and saying things that didn't make any sense. Eventually, he hit rock bottom. Ended up in a ditch, then the hospital and then rehab.

Joe tells his story over and over to high school students and anyone else who will listen. He made it out of that sticky web, but it wasn't easy. He would tell you that drugs are a demon he battles every day.

I often wonder what would have happened if Joe didn't have the support of his family and friends.

Today, he's married to a wonderful woman who, like him, counsels drug addicts.

It's good to see Joe's smiling eyes, and it's good to see wrinkles hug the outer corners. As the years pass and the wrinkles appear, it means he's beating the demon – one day at a time.

Bill (Yearbook post)

Gina,

To a very special girl that I think about a lot and I will never forget you as long as I live. I have many memories about you that I wouldn't trade for the world, and I'm sure you have some memories too and I hope you never forget them. You made this past summer something very special and something to always remember and I want to thank you for that. I'm sorry what we had together had to end but it seems like it's been for the best. I'm really glad that you and Mike found each other and I hope your relationship always lasts. I don't know Mike very well but it seems like you two were made for each other and I'm really happy for you. You deserve the very best that life has to offer and I hope you always get it. Best wishes and please take good care of yourself.

Love, Bill

....

I dated Bill the summer before I started dating Mike. I learned how to make out and French kiss hard and deep. We never went the whole way. We were both too scared. And while we knew we liked each other a lot, maybe not quite enough to go that far. So we had a summer romance filled with fun days and steamy nights.

I was the one who broke it off. School started and we weren't spending as much time together, and I realized that I didn't care that we weren't spending as much time together. And then I started to look at Mike and, well, it was only a matter of time.

Just being near Mike made my heart tingle. It never tingled with Bill. And then one day Bill came around the corner at school and saw me talking to Mike. Later that day, he mentioned it and said how I had a smile on my face that he had never seen before. He told me that he wished I had smiled at him like that. That was the day I broke up with him. I think we both knew it was coming. The summer was over.

Keith (Yearbook post)

Gina,

To a really sweet girl who has a nice personality. Keep up the good looks and keep working hard and you'll go far. See you over the summer.

Love, Keith

....

Keith was the first boy I ever kissed. It was in sixth grade and we were playing Spin the Bottle in my girlfriend's garage. There were eight of us, four boys and four girls. We sat in a circle — boy, girl, boy, girl. If the bottle pointed at someone of the same gender, you kissed the person to their left. I got to go first because I picked the longest blade of grass. I spun the empty bottle of Budweiser that we dug out of the trash. When the bottle stopped spinning, it was pointing at Keith.

I wasn't sure if I was supposed to open my mouth when we kissed. The girls and I had talked about it earlier that day when we planned to meet up with the boys in Becky's garage, but I realized we hadn't made a decision. Now I was first and everyone would probably follow whatever I did. I thought my heart was going to explode out of my chest. It pounded so fast it scared me. Even when I gave a violin recital, and I was always nervous at those, my heart didn't pound like this.

I sat cross-legged on the cold cement. Keith looked at me and he didn't move. The others were egging me on. I finally got up enough courage and got on my knees and wiggled over to Keith. I decided I wasn't going to open my mouth. I gave him a quick peck and everyone ooed and ahhed.

Whenever I'm with someone at a bar and they buy a bottle of Budweiser, I remember that day so many years ago. And I also remember Becky's mom catching us kissing after only a few spins. She chased us all out of the garage and sent the boys home. It wasn't the last time we played Spin the Bottle, but it was the last time at Becky's house.

Keith followed in his dad's footsteps and became an eye doctor. When he joined his dad's practice, they built a new office with state-of-the-art technology and equipment. Keith married a nurse that he met in school. They have five kids – two sets of twin girls and a boy.

Frank (Yearbook post)

Gina,

To a really neat girl I've known for awhile now. Thanks for trying to keep me awake during Period 6. I don't think I would have made it through school without your help. Good luck in college. I know you'll do great, you always do.

Love, Frank

....

Frank was forever falling asleep in class. But I would, too, if I were stocking grocery store shelves until 2 in the morning. By the time he got home and to sleep it was almost time to get back up. School started at 7:40. But Frank's family needed the money. He never talked about his dad and I got the feeling that he left when Frank was really young.

His mom worked at the mini mart in town during the day and cleaned office buildings at night. He had three sisters who weren't old enough to work. He told me one time how embarrassed he was that his family got food stamps and that he qualified for a reduced lunch at school. He hated being poor.

I was so happy that he got a college scholarship. Actually, he was offered several. Despite falling asleep and not doing his homework half the time he was one of the smartest kids in our class. In fact, he was nudged out by Keith for salutatorian by tenths of a point.

Frank decided to attend the local university so he could continue to help out at home. He was one of those kids who you never felt got a break. But that changed in college. A professor took him under his wing and mentored him. I guess he saw potential in Frank and wanted to help him. Turned out that Frank earned his undergrad in business and went on to get his MBA.

He's doing quite well from what Mom tells me. And she sent me a newspaper clipping of Frank starting a program in our high school for kids interested in business. He got other business leaders in the community to help mentor the kids. The students set up a store in the school and were learning the ins and outs of running a business.

And all this from a kid I constantly had to nudge to keep awake in period 6. It makes me smile.

Sue, aka Tigger (Yearbook post)

Gina, to my dearest and closest friend. You are an amazing person and I love you so much! Always remember the good times we shared, especially the wild parties at Jeremy's. I wish you nothing but the best in everything you do. I know that you will go far. Thanks for always being there for me. I will always be here for you. You can call me anytime anywhere. Remember, soul sisters forever! You are an incredible person and friend. I love you, Tig

....

Sue, aka Tig for Tigger, is my best friend. She's the only friend from high school that I've kept in touch with. And that's mostly because she made the effort long before I started to carry some of the water.

After college, Sue went to paralegal school. I tried to talk her into going to law school with me, but she wasn't up to putting in another three years. She got a job as a paralegal for an attorney. That's how she met her husband. He was an attorney, too. Turned out he liked women. A lot. Sue caught him screwing their neighbor when she came home for lunch one day. The only thing good that came out of that marriage was Chloe.

When Sue asked me to be Chloe's godmother, I was speechless. I love Chloe as if she were mine. I always thought I would have kids. I wanted kids. It just never happened. Just like finding the right guy to spend my life with never happened. I had been close a few times, but there was always something that stopped me from taking that final step. It wasn't that I was scared, more like unsure that I loved him enough.

So as the years passed my work became my life. And, now that I'm pushing 40 and I know that time is running out, I'm thinking about having the baby I've always wanted -- even if it means doing it alone. I see how Sue and Chloe are and I want that, too. I know it won't be easy being a single mother, but I'm used to things not being easy.

Jeremy (Yearbook post)

Gina,

To a really nice girl that I always can hear over where I sit. You're one of the good girls in this school. Take care of Mike and remember all the great times we had hanging out.

Good luck, Bean

....

Thanks, Jeremy. You were just as loud. Maybe louder. Jeremy was the tallest guy I knew. He was 6-foot, 7-inches and the star of our basketball team. He was also thin. That's how he got the nickname "Bean." I think three of my steps equaled one of his. He also had perfect teeth. His dad was a dentist.

Jeremy was my boyfriend's best friend. Mike and I played matchmaker and fixed Jeremy up with Ellen for the prom. They dated the rest of that senior year and summer, but when Jeremy went away to play basketball for a college in the Midwest and Ellen went to a private school in Vermont, that pretty much killed that.

In high school, Jeremy had the most amazing parties. His parents were away most weekends. They had a place at the beach and one in the mountains. We'd hang out at Jeremy's and drink beer. I got my first carpet burn when Mike and I made out on the floor in Jeremy's room.

Jeremy went to dental school and joined his dad's practice. He married a girl he met in college. I've met Teresa once or twice over the years and she seems super nice. She's not tall, though. There must be a foot difference between them. I don't think she can kiss him even if she stands on her tip-toes. I think they have a couple of kids.

Alicia (Yearbook post)

Gina,

To a really super friend and a great person to be with. Never forget all of the fun we had playing Barbie's when we were kids. I'm not good at words like you are but I hope you realize how much I value our friendship. Take care of yourself and I wish you the best of luck in everything you do.

Love always, Alicia

....

Alicia and I spent many afternoons playing Barbie's. She lived down the street, and I'd cart my Barbie house and my Barbie car and my Barbie case over to her house. She had a big bedroom, and there was lots of space on her green shag carpet to spread everything out. We spent entire afternoons pretending.

Alicia and I vowed that when we grew up, we'd get an apartment together. Of course, we'd have fabulous jobs and fabulous boyfriends who would turn into fabulous husbands. And we'd live in fabulous homes and have fabulous kids. Everything would be fabulous.

Talk about a colossal fail because it wasn't too fabulous for Alicia -- in fact, what happened to Alicia was devastating and changed her life forever.

She was running alone at dusk through a cemetery on the edge of town and was raped by a man that had apparently hidden behind the mausoleum. It was a weeknight, and the place was empty.

They never found the rapist, and Alicia never went running again. She became a hermit, afraid to leave her house.

Whenever I'm home, I visit her. She spends her days putting puzzles together and I always make sure I bring her a few new ones. I get so depressed when I visit Alicia and then I feel guilty for being so depressed. The Alicia I knew was in love with life. She wanted to do things and go places and, of course, have a fabulous life. I tried talking to her about the rape but the minute I mention it she screams for me to leave. So I stopped.

I hate the prison walls she has built up around her. I hate that the doctors have not been able to help her. I hate that she doesn't have the fabulous life she always wanted and deserves. Mostly, I hate the guy who brutally raped her and left her for dead. She wasn't found until the next day when a train of cars snaked through the narrow roads of the cemetery on the way to a burial site. The men driving the hearse saw her as they passed the mausoleum. She wasn't moving. They thought she was dead. Turned out they were more right than wrong.

Eric (Yearbook post)

Gina,

To a fun girl I met my junior year in high school. Keep that great personality and friendly smile and you'll go far. Never forget all of Mrs. Hoffman's crazy stories and how we got her to waste entire class periods talking about her childhood. Good luck in college and with Mike.

Best, Eric

....

Eric loved history. He ended up becoming a history teacher for a school in Rhode Island. He was also a Civil War re-enactor. Mom sent me a newspaper clipping one time that had a photo of him dressed in a blue and gray uniform standing beside a woman in a massive hoop skirt. Despite his bushy sideburns, I could tell it was him.

Eric was great at getting our English teacher, Mrs. Hoffman, to tell us stories from her childhood. Whenever we didn't want to work in class, we'd get Eric to get Mrs. Hoffman started. She was like a wind-up toy. Once you wound her up, she just kept going. Eric saved my ass more than once in her class.

I can't picture Eric as a teacher. But I can totally see the whole re-enactor thing. He was always passionate about the Civil War and could describe every single battle in detail. Come to think of it, he was a lot like Hoffman in that regard. Get him on a topic he loved and he wouldn't shut up.

About the Author

Buffy Andrews is an author, blogger, journalist and social media maven. Oh – and wife, mother, sister and friend.

By day she's a journalist, leading an award-winning staff at the York Daily Record/Sunday News, where she is Assistant Managing Editor of Features and Niche Publications and social media coordinator.

You will find her on a plethora of social networking sites, from Twitter and Facebook to RebelMouse and NewHive. She loves social media and loves to connect with her fans via the various platforms.

In addition to her writing blog, Buffy's Write Zone, she maintains a social media blog, Buffy's World.

She is also a newspaper and magazine columnist and writes middle-grade, young adult and women's fiction.

Buffy says that some of her fiction ideas pop into her head at the most inopportune times. She has jumped out of the shower to write an idea down, scribbled all over church bulletins and meeting agendas. She said she has fallen in love with each one of her characters and she is thankful they came into her life and can't wait to share them with you.

She lives in southcentral Pennsylvania with her husband, Tom; two sons, Zach and Micah; and wheaten cairn terrier Kakita. She is grateful for their love and support and for reminding her of what's most important in life.

When she isn't writing, she's running or trying to play golf. She loves all things Disney and would love to spend a night (or week) in Cinderella's Castle.

Once you get to know Buffy, you will quickly see that she is a big believer in giving back. She has designated that 5 percent of the proceeds from her books (ebook and print) will be given to charity. So when you buy her books, you will also be helping others.

Acknowledgements

I've dreamed of this moment forever, and now that it's here, I'm not sure where to begin. There are so many people I'd like to thank, so many people who encouraged me as I pursued this dream. They include family and friends, colleagues and teachers. They pushed me when I needed to be pushed, encouraged me when I needed to be encouraged. And, when the mountain seemed too steep to climb, they reminded me that often the things we want most in life are the hardest to achieve.

I especially thank God for his love and understanding. He has been with me on this journey and I'm grateful for his guidance.

I thank Beth Vrabel, my awesome friend and fellow author, whose honesty and thoughtful editing challenged me to make my work better.

I thank my best friends Robin Bohanan and Kris Ort for their love and incredible friendship. We've been together a long time, girls, and I love you both very much.

I thank Sharon Kirchoff, my biggest cheerleader, who loves my work as much as I do -- maybe even more!

I thank the entire Limitless team, an incredible group of people that I've been blessed to have had the opportunity to work with.

I thank my sisters Dawn Beakler, Cindy Andrews and Tania Nade, for a lifetime of love and laughs.

And, lastly, I thank my husband Tom, and my sons, Zach and Micah, for the wonderful life we share. I love you guys bunches and bunches.

Facebook:
https://www.facebook.com/buffy.andrews

Twitter:
https://twitter.com/buffyandrews

Website:
www.authorbuffyandrews.com/

Goodreads:
www.goodreads.com/user/show/7370309-buffy-andrews

Blog:
http://buffyswritezone.blogspot.com/

Tumbler:
http://buffyandrews.tumblr.com/

Pinterest:
http://pinterest.com/buffyandrews/

26075740R00165

Made in the USA
Lexington, KY
15 September 2013